Permanently Pucked

CHICAGO RACKETEERS
BOOK FOUR

EMMA FOXX

Copyright © 2024 Blake Wilder Books, LLC

All rights reserved.

No part of this book may be reproduced in any form or by any electronic or mechanical means, including information storage and retrieval systems, without written permission from the author, except for the use of brief quotations in a book review.

Cover design by Qamber Designs

About The Book

I don't do casual hookups. Never have. Not even with the three supposed-to-be one-night stands I had six months ago.

They all turned into the loves of my life.

But now I know *exactly* what to do with the three hot guys I met at that serendipitous hockey game. Love them. Forever. At least that's the plan.

Our house is truly a home, the naked-times are better than any dirty romance I've ever read…or written…and our relationship is rock solid.

As long as we can take our foursome to four plus a bundle of joy without any of my guys deciding that our unconventional approach to family is just a little more than he bargained for.

Permanently Pucked

By
Emma Foxx

CHAPTER 1
Nathan

I AM one minute away from finding out if my life is going to change forever.

Literally. The timer on the counter is ticking off the seconds.

And that life change is going to affect three other people. Who are all crowded into my bathroom with me at the moment.

This isn't exactly how I ever pictured getting life altering news.

Of course, I never pictured getting *this* particular news in my life at all.

I've seen these moments in movies and television shows. The ones where the couple has the pregnancy test beside them, and they're waiting for the timer to ring and tell them the happy—or terrible, depending on their perspective and the situation—news.

But for me, I've always known I couldn't have children, so I've somehow automatically put that all into the category of Things That Happen to Other People.

Like flying in economy, or shopping at Wal-Mart.

Suddenly Danielle laughs quietly, and I swing around from where I've paced to the door again.

She's sitting on the counter next to the four pregnancy tests I bought just under an hour ago. When the love of my life said she needed a test to see if we're going to have a baby, of course I bought four. That's reasonable. I almost bought ten. But I want to be sure about this. My heart rate hasn't slowed since her words sunk in and...fuck...the hope keeps growing.

I need to get it together. Because if these tests *aren't* positive, I'm going to be a mess.

I want this so much it's actually concerning me. I knew, deep down, that I wanted this to happen for us, eventually. My girlfriend having two other boyfriends does have some perks. But I thought it would be down the road. Danielle's young. I had no idea when she'd be ready for kids and I was not going to push.

But now...I swallow. I definitely need to get it together. This could be a stomach bug.

Right now, it would be easy to believe that she's just ill. She's pale, and her eyes are red-rimmed, and she hasn't said a word for nearly ten minutes. She's just been following Michael's instructions for the tests and to eat some crackers and drink some water.

Michael is leaning against the counter next to her. Crew is sitting on the edge of the huge jacuzzi tub across from her. They also look concerned by her suddenly hysterical-sounding laughter.

"You okay?" Michael asks her.

She gives him a sweet smile. "Yep."

Michael moves to stand right in front of her. He lifts a hand and cups her cheek. "We're right here."

She nods and squeezes his wrist. Then she looks at Crew and finally at me. "I'm really okay."

I start to reply, but the timer on my phone goes off and we all jump.

I immediately reach for the closest test, the one she took first. I hold my breath and look down.

My heart falls to my stomach. My chest tightens and for a second I have a hard time swallowing.

Finally I choke out, "Negative."

Fuck.

Okay, this isn't the end of the world. It's not the end of this journey. It wasn't even the start. This was all a surprise. None of us were planning on a pregnancy right now. Michael and I have only just proposed to her. We're just getting started.

It's okay.

Still, I'm so much more disappointed than I'd expected.

Danielle's head whips around to look at me.

"What?" she asks.

I hold out the stick. "It's negative." My voice is tight.

She takes the test from me and looks up at Michael, as if needing his confirmation. Or hoping he'll make it all okay. "Negative?"

Michael looks at the test, then puts his hands on her thighs and squeezes. He gives her a nod. "Negative."

As much as my chest hurts, it's nothing compared to what I feel when Danielle's disappointed gaze meets mine again. She takes my hand. "Nathan–"

She's breaking my heart. My girl wanted this. She wanted to be pregnant.

Fuck, what am I supposed to do about that? I'd take her into the bedroom right now and knock her up this minute if I could.

Hell, Michael and Crew can. That's exactly what we should—

"How does a plus sign mean negative?" Crew asks.

He's holding another of the sticks.

We all look at him.

"What?" Michael asks.

Crew holds it up. There's a bright pink plus sign on this one. "A plus sign is a negative test? That's stupid."

Michael grabs it from him and looks at the stick. Then he grabs the box.

But they don't have to say anything else. That fucking bubble of hope is back in my chest. Just like that. Dammit.

Danielle and my fingers collide as we reach for another of the tests.

She looks up at me. We just stare at each other for a long moment.

We both want this. So much. I want to have this with her. I can't create the actual baby with her, but I sure as hell can make a *family* with her.

This beautiful, sweet creature has brought love and life back into my world. She has no idea what she means to me.

I watch her swallow.

I give her a smile.

And when she smiles back, I feel my heart expand and I know in that moment...she's pregnant. It makes no sense, but I just *know*.

We're going to do this. And it's going to be amazing.

She nods, as if reading my thoughts, and we look down at the same time.

"Positive," she says quietly.

"Pos–" I have to stop and clear my throat. "Positive."

Jesus. I feel a little weak in the knees. I'm overwhelmed.

Michael picks up the last test. "Positive," he says.

Danielle's eyes fill with tears and Michael drops the test to take her face in his hands, kissing her tenderly. "I love you, Dani," he says against her lips. "I love you so much."

She hugs him tightly. "I love you, too."

"You've given me...everything," he says thickly. "I adore you. I cherish you. All of me is yours, always."

"God." A tear slips down her cheek. "This is like a dream. I'm so happy, Michael."

He kisses her again, then steps out of the way and I'm there, crowding in, my mouth on hers, scooping my hands under her ass, and pulling her off the counter. She wraps herself around me, our bodies plastered together.

I drag my mouth to her ear. "Danielle...I love you." I feel tears stinging my eyes and I pull back to look at her. "Thank you," I tell her sincerely.

I know she knows what I mean. I'm thanking her for loving me in spite of my cold exterior, my gruffness, my resistance to the relationship around us that makes her so happy, to opening up and letting them all in. I'm thanking her for the patience it took to let me get to this place where I know this is all right and what I want.

And I'm thanking her for letting me be a father to this baby that I want so fucking much.

She hugs me tightly. "I love you, Nathan."

I want to just hold her indefinitely, but there is someone else in the room who is a part of this and while I know Danielle needs to share this with him, even more I know Crew needs her to ground him in this crazy moment. He's not fully on the marriage-and-kids train yet.

I set her on her feet and turn her to face her third boyfriend.

He looks dazed, but he immediately gathers her into his arms and puts his face against her neck.

She runs her fingers through his hair. "Say something," she tells him softly.

He doesn't pull back. He seems to hug her even tighter. "Well...holy shit."

She gives a soft laugh. "I love you, Crew."

"I love you too, Dani girl."

She's quiet for a moment, stroking her hands down his back. Then she asks him, "Will you teach our baby to play hockey?"

Crew shakes his head. "No."

I frown and glance at Michael. He also looks concerned. We know that Crew is feeling overwhelmed by a lot of what's going on in our little unit. We've all just moved in together and there are still adjustments being made to sharing a living space twenty-four-seven. Michael and I have proposed, Crew's not ready for that. And now...a baby.

We're willing to accept that we all have different relationships with Danielle and we don't all have to be at the same place at the same time. As long as she's happy.

But if that starts to change, I *will* intervene. No one hurts Danielle. No one.

She pulls back to look at Crew.

But he's smiling faintly now. "I'm going to teach our baby to *win* hockey."

The tension leaves my shoulders. *Our* baby.

Okay. That's more like it.

I don't have to kick Crew McNeill's ass today.

But there's a lot of time between now and 'til death do us part.

CHAPTER 2
Dani

"I'M GOING TO THROW UP," I tell my best friend, taking a deep breath and pressing my hand to my stomach. I concentrate on breathing through my nose.

"It's okay to be nervous," Luna says. "But you *cannot* throw up. This dress is just too gorgeous. The wedding dress gods will be angry if you sully it."

That makes me laugh softly. "I'm not nervous."

I'm not. I'm excited. *Thrilled*. I'm marrying Michael and Nathan today in a commitment ceremony, surrounded by our family and dearest friends, including my boyfriend, Crew, who is our best man. I'm marrying two men who have loved me better than I could have ever imagined, who care for me and protect me and who always hear me and my needs.

After a whirlwind search for a venue, during which Nathan rejected a dozen options, we settled on a space with an ivy covered brick courtyard with burbling fountains and an explosion of plants for the ceremony, and an intimate and moody dining space inside, with a soaring two-story atrium so that we can see the stars when the sun sets. It's actually the home of one of Nathan's billionaire friends, who is currently in Dubai for six months and offered Nathan the use for our wedding.

Luna and I are in one of the bedroom suites, which is decorated in a soothing palette of ivory and sage, with lots of texture. The wallpaper is a fabric toile, and I feel like a princess standing in front of the full-length mirror, staring at myself in my chiffon gown with a sweetheart bodice and balloon sleeves. The skirt is loose and flowing and we've left my hair down to tumble in loose curls to match the ease of the skirt. My face is pale but my eyes are bright with happiness. While the waist of the skirt is narrow, it's not tight. I didn't expect to feel both so beautiful and nauseous all at the same time. I also didn't plan to have a baby, but here we are and I'm over the moon.

But nauseous.

"I'm going to throw up because I'm pregnant. I can't help it." I clutch my waist.

I'm only eight weeks along and I'm right in the throes of morning sickness. But today it seems to have spilled over into morning, noon, and night sickness. Maybe Luna is right. Maybe I am nervous. Not because this isn't what I want, but because it's exactly what I *do* want. To see Michael and Nathan stand up and commit to me forever has tears filling my eyes.

"No, you are absolutely not going to be sick," Luna tells me, as if she can will my vomiting away. "Just forget about it. Not happening. Do you want some water?"

I nod, afraid if I speak anymore, I'll lose the fight. I press my fingers under my eyes, not wanting the tears to fall and ruin my makeup.

"Do you want me to get your mom?"

I shake my head quietly. "No. Absolutely not." Maybe that's also why my emotions are running high. My parents are here for the ceremony, but only reluctantly. They'll stay through dinner, but leave before the reception morphs into a full-blown party. Their acceptance of my poly relationship has been slow, with its ups and downs. They're trying to understand and be supportive, but they can't quite mask their concern. They don't know I'm pregnant, because the guys and I all agreed that we would wait until I'm past my first trimester before we share our news. Luna knows because I told her I thought I might be pregnant when I first realized I had missed my period. And because, as amazing as my men are, a girl definitely needs a girlfriend sometimes, and this is one of those times.

Luna hands me a glass filled with sparkling water. "The bubbles will be good for your tummy." She's wearing a mama-bear expression. "I can't believe your parents. I'd love to tell them exactly how I feel about their manufactured drama. They're being gross."

That makes me laugh softly after I sip the water carefully. "They're here because they love me. That's enough, or it's going to have to be. But Michael's whole family is also here, and your family, and Val, and all of the Racketeers, both players and staff, and it's *amazing*. It's almost perfect."

It would be truly perfect if my parents really were happy for me and if Crew was marrying me as well. But my sweet best friend is in a different place, and I'm respecting that his timeframe isn't the same as mine. I'd marry him, too, in a heartbeat if he was ready though.

"I can't believe I actually have a plus three for this wedding," Luna says with a grin, checking her hair in the mirror. She's wearing a blush bridesmaid dress in a similar style to mine, with drop sleeves. "The last two weddings I attended, I went to solo. Now I'm drowning in dates. I love it."

"I'm so happy for you." I am ecstatic that Luna has found her men. Owen, Alexsei, and Cam all meet different needs for her and love her unconditionally. It's been fabulous to watch my bestie falling in love times three. "It will be your turn to get married next," I tell her in a sing-song voice, shooting her a grin.

My stomach feels better. I take another sip of water.

Luna pauses in the middle of retouching her lipstick and shoots me a look in the mirror. "If you throw the bouquet my way, I won't dodge it. Let's put it that way."

"Oooh," I say, excited. "Then you can have a baby, too, and we'll raise our kids together and…"

She's laughing and waving her hands. "Oh my god, Dani, slow down! Let's get you married and leave me to just enjoy my so-new-it's-just-been-all-of-a-hot-minute-relationship for a while."

"Fine." I give her a soft smile and try to tame an errant curl in the mirror.

There's a knock on the bedroom door.

"I'll get it," Luna says. "If it's Nathan or Michael I'll get rid of them."

"You won't be able to keep Nathan out of here if he's at that door," I tell her with a grin. "Though he did promise me he'd stay away. I want him to see me for the first time when I walk down the aisle."

Luna cracks the door open. "Lorraine, hi. Come on in."

It's Michael's mom. I turn and the look of love and tenderness on her face makes me tear up all over again. When she moves toward me with her arms open, I immediately shift into her hug and wrap my arms tightly around her. It's a mother's hug, even if it's not my own mom.

She pulls back, and holding my hands, lifts my arms out. "Let me look at you. You're stunning, Dani. My son is a lucky man."

"I'm a lucky woman. Michael is a really good man and an amazing partner."

Lorraine lowers our arms and squeezes my hands. "He's going to be an amazing father as well, isn't he? You're pregnant, aren't you?"

I don't know what to say. My cheeks flush. I don't think Michael would have told her but… she looks very certain.

"No one told me," she reassures me. "But I had six of my own, remember? I recognize the look. Excitement, nerves, and a little bit of nausea." She gestures to the sparkling water. "It will be our little secret." She cups my cheeks. "Just make sure you keep eating small bites of something all day. Don't let yourself go hungry or it will get worse."

I nod. "I won't. Thank you."

She cups my face lovingly. "I'm so thrilled. You're giving my son everything he's always wanted and it's even more than he could have ever imagined." She gives me a smile that's so full of love I suck in a breath. "Thank you, my sweet girl."

I blink rapidly against the threatening tears. "I've never been happier," I tell her sincerely.

"I'm so glad." Lorraine hugs me again, then steps back. "I should get back out to Clayton. I wouldn't let him come in, though he wanted to see you."

"How is he feeling?" Michael's father had two heart attacks back to back recently.

"He's good. He's thrilled about today, too. But he might have to skip the reception to rest."

"I'm so glad you're both here. It means the world to us."

"I wouldn't miss it for anything. Welcome to the family, Danielle."

She pats Luna on the cheek on her way to the door, then leaves.

I feel much calmer and my stomach has settled down. "Can you fix my eye makeup?"

There's another knock on the door. "Who is it?" Luna calls out.

"It's me."

My heart seems to skip a beat. It's Crew.

"Go away," Luna tells her brother.

"Let me in, sis." His voice sounds cheerful. "I need to see Dani real quick."

"It's okay," I tell her. "I want to see him."

Luna opens the door and eyes her brother. "Don't make her cry."

I can't see him but I hear Crew scoff. "Why would I make her cry? Look, I have presents."

"Come in," I call out.

Crew comes through the door and my breath catches. He looks incredibly handsome in his tuxedo, two beautiful gift boxes in his hands. He draws up short, his eyes wide as he takes me in.

He blows out a breath. "Damn, baby, you look gorgeous."

"Thank you." I pose a little, hand on my hip. "You don't look so bad yourself."

"I'll be right back," Luna says, ducking out into the hallway with her phone in her hand. She gently closes the door behind her.

"Apparently, there is some wedding tradition where the groom is supposed to give the bride a gift. So, one from Nathan." He lifts his right hand. "One from Michael." He lifts his left hand.

"Oh, wow, I had no idea that was a thing. Which one should I open first?"

"Nathan," Crew says immediately. His eyes are twinkling. "Because he's the oldest." He passes me the gift box. "And the grumpiest."

I give a giggle. "He's getting less grumpy every day."

"That is true."

I slip the card out of the envelope resting on a Tiffany blue box.

"Should I leave?" Crew asks.

"What? No, of course not. Unless you want to leave."

He shakes his head. "No." He shoves his free hand in his pocket like he doesn't know what to do with it. "I want to be here for you. For everything."

That gives me pause. I lean in and kiss him softly. "I love you."

"I love you too."

The note from Nathan is very Nathan-like. Short and to the point.

I can't wait to call you my wife. I love you.

I clasp the card to my chest. God, I love Nathan so much. From the minute I met him, he has swept me away in a storm of passion, devotion, and love. Sometimes it's overwhelming, but in the very best way.

There's an elegant diamond bracelet in the box. I gasp at how beautiful it is. It's more Nathan's style than mine, but I know he shows love with extravagant gifts. This whole wedding, which is a little over-the-top, is an expression of Nathan's love for me.

"Let me put it on you." Crew takes the bracelet and clasps it around my wrist. He raises my hand to his lips and kisses it. "It's going to be hard for Doc to top diamonds. See what he's got up his sleeve, sweetheart."

"It's not a competition."

"Says you." Crew grins.

I pluck out Michael's note when Crew hands me the second box.

You're everything I've been waiting for.
And we lived happily ever after.
I love you,
Michael

It's a hardback book with gold foil and sprayed edges of the greatest love poems ever written. I hug it to my chest with a heartfelt sigh. Michael gets me and he understands me sometimes even before I understand myself. I love him so deeply.

"Now I know what I'm up against," Crew says. "I'm feeling hot-air balloon when we get married someday."

That makes me laugh. "I don't think so. This girl's feet are staying firmly on the ground."

"That's not what happened last night." He tugs on one of my curls. "I seem to remember your feet on Nathan's shoulders."

"Stop." I blush. In spite of the morning sickness early in the day, at night I've been extra needy when it comes to sex. Fortunately, I have three guys happy to indulge me, even if Crew is being oddly cautious.

I don't know if it's the pregnancy or the upcoming commitment ceremony, but he's been uncharacteristically tentative in bed for the last two weeks. Like I might break.

I'm not going to worry about that right now though. Especially since he nuzzles into my neck and kisses me. "Nope. Never going to stop."

We're kissing passionately, Michael's book pressed between us, when Luna returns. "Break it up. It's time to walk down the aisle."

Crew pulls back and gives me a wink. "I'll see you out there."

I lift my hand to wipe my lipstick from his mouth. "See you soon."

When he slips through the door, Luna eyes me. "You okay?"

I nod again, throat tight. I know she's asking about Crew and how a family of four can operate out of tandem, but I don't want to talk about it right now. I just want to get married to the two men who are on the same page as me at this moment. We're still Cookie & Co. Even when things change around us, even if our timeline is a little wacky, even if we add one little baby to our 'company', it's still us at the center.

"I'm fantastic. Look what Nathan gave me." I hold up my wrist. "And this is from Michael." I lift the book to my nose and breathe deeply. I love the smell of books. Then I set it down on the vanity table next to my makeup bag. "I'm ready."

When the double doors are opened for me by two of the Racketeers players, Blake Wilder and Jack Hayes, looking dashing in their tuxedos, I take a deep breath and just take in the sight before me, trying to absorb it all.

The courtyard is an explosion of plants, ivy, and floral arrangements. The Chippendale chairs are in tidy rows on either side of the petal strewn aisle, filled with all our friends and family. Everyone has turned and is watching me with big smiles, Luna reaching the end of the aisle and taking her place as my maid of honor.

Nathan and Michael are waiting at the end of that aisle, standing tall and straight, side by side. Crew is next to them.

Happily ever after.

That's it right there. Those three men. All I'll ever want or need. It's all mine.

My nerves and my stomach quiet in that pause, that hushed moment of anticipation, as I take it all in, wanting to commit it to memory as I clutch my gorgeous bouquet of hellebore, garden roses, and dahlias in varying shades of white and ivory. The music swells, and Blake tilts his head, encouraging me to go in. Jack gives a flourish with his arm and it makes me laugh softly.

My steps are steady and sure as I walk down the aisle, at first glancing around at our guests, awed and overjoyed at the display of emotions on various faces. Val is dabbing her eyes with a tissue, clasping Stanford's hand, who has a nurse on his opposite side. The Racketeers players, including Luna's boyfriend, are all sitting together with their coaches, a mass of muscle and grins. Michael's whole family is smiling, Lorraine giving me an encouraging nod. The McNeills are there, next to my parents, who look a little shell-shocked. My mother is crying and my father is stoically staring at me.

Our bookstore employees are all sitting together with Owen's son Brady and his girlfriend Lydia. Elise gives me a look of appreciation and mouths, "so hot," to me, which makes me giggle.

Then I only have eyes for my guys.

When I reach the last few feet of the aisle, our gazes meet and my heart is so happy I blink away the tears that suddenly appear.

Nathan also has tears in his eyes that he makes no move to hide or wipe away. His nostrils are flaring, his jaw set.

Michael is grinning from ear-to-ear, shaking his head a little like he can't believe his good fortune.

They both look devastatingly handsome. They always do, but somehow looking at them now, knowing that in a few minutes they will be my *husbands*, makes everything from the shape of Nathan's mouth to the crinkles by Michael's eyes even more attractive and more dear. It's all mine. Every inch of their bodies and souls are *mine*. Forever. And this formal, beautiful ceremony announcing that to everyone who matters to us, makes it so big and real and amazing. The surge of possessiveness and love I feel makes me feel a little dizzy.

Crew is off to the side a little, hands clasped in front of him, shoulders squared back. The way my heart fills looking at him makes the stinging in my eyes and the surge of love and possessiveness even stronger.

He's mine too. We don't *need* a ceremony to know it.

But God, in this moment, I so wish he was standing up here with us, making this promise too.

I swallow hard and hand my bouquet to Luna, then reach out. Nathan takes one hand and Michael takes the other, both of them giving me a squeeze. We move into the center to face the officiant.

"We are gathered here today..."

The officiant is one of Michael's cousins, Isaac, and as he talks, I see his mouth moving, but I barely hear the words. My focus is on the two hands holding mine. I glance over at Nathan and he gives me a look with such intensity that I feel my cheeks flush, and I squeeze his hand tightly. Then when I glance over at Michael, he raises his eyebrows up and down in a move that is so uncharacteristic I grin at him. He's shifting on the balls of his feet like he has too much energy to stay still.

I force myself to tune into the officiant.

"We have this wonderful opportunity today to show love in one of its many forms," Isaac says. "The writer Aberjhani said that, 'This fire that we call Loving is too strong for human minds. But just right for human souls.' Love can't be comprehended with logic, it can't be explained, and we can't force it to fit the expectations of others or society. We must let it live where it sparked, in the sanctity of our hearts, fanning it with devotion, commitment, and reverence. It takes mindful attendance to keep a flame burning bright and Danielle, Michael, and Nathan, as you stand here today before your family and friends, you're making a promise to each other to always tend to your fire, to love with dedication and an open heart and mind."

Everything he's saying resonates deeply with me.

I plan to love my guys with dedication and an open heart for the rest of my life.

Michael lifts my hand to his lips and presses a kiss on my knuckles.

Nathan clears his throat. When I look over at him, there is a single tear running down his cheek. I lean over and kiss his cheek next to the tear. He meets my gaze and smiles.

I'm the happiest I've ever been in my life.

Only one thing could make today better.

Crew marrying me too.

CHAPTER 3
Crew

HOW THE FUCK is a guy supposed to feel when he's watching his girlfriend get married to his two best friends?

Confused is the right answer, because damn, I'm all over the place emotionally.

Dani looks beautiful. The blushing bride. The *pregnant* blushing bride. I'm very aware when I look at her that she is carrying a baby. Our baby. Cookie & Co. It might be mine. Or it might be Michael's. I suspect Michael's, but does that really matter? Not with what we've said we all are to each other.

It's a lot of responsibility, a baby, marriage, a home, forever.

I want that. All of it, with Dani. Hell, with Nate and Doc too.

But at the same time, it freaks me the fuck out. I can barely feed myself and manage my finances, how the hell can I be a husband, a father? The other guys love to give me a hard time about my snack food choices and lack of housekeeping. Then there's hockey. It's my career, my dream, and we're right in the middle of playoffs. It doesn't feel like there is enough of me to go around.

Or if there is, what my role is here now.

I concentrate on standing still and not rocking back on my heels and fidgeting the way I really want to.

I'm damn happy to see Nathan and Michael commit to our girl. They want this. She deserves it.

But I still feel a mix of emotions I don't exactly know how to describe.

Or maybe I can. I feel like I'm letting them down.

That's what it is. I don't like naming it, but I can't avoid it at this moment.

That gorgeous, sweet, loving, amazing woman standing five feet from me wants me. I don't always understand why, but I believe it. She'd be thrilled beyond measure if I stepped forward and said, "Me too," and added myself in as a husband and not just the best man.

Me *not* standing there with her, vowing alongside Michael and Nathan, disappoints her. I know it does.

She's been more supportive of my feelings on this than she probably should be, but she loves me and I never forget how lucky I am that's true. But this isn't exactly what she wants.

I also feel like I'm disappointing Nathan and Michael. And their opinions of me matter. I respect them. Hell, I love them. We are a family. Of course letting them down makes me feel like shit.

"Do you, Nathan, take this woman, to be your wife, until death do you part?"

"I do," Nathan says in a strong, confident voice, even as there are tears in his eyes.

The raw emotion he's allowing everyone to see is touching as hell. He deserves to be part of a family after everything he's lost in his life.

"Danielle," he says, cupping her cheek with one hand. "I always thought I'd be alone, that my fate was to be a bachelor forever, and I was fine with that. Then you walked into my life, and in an instant, I rewrote everything that I knew about the rest of my life. You bring me joy, a purpose, contentment, and a love I don't even deserve. You complete me, and I will spend the rest of forever making sure you're taken care of in every way possible. I love you, Danielle, with my whole grumpy heart."

Dani gives a soft laugh. "Nathan, I love your grumpy heart. I love how strong you are and how safe you make me feel. I love knowing that you'll be there for me no matter what and that I can bring you happiness. We're a family now."

I don't feel jealousy watching them, hearing their vows of dedication and love. I'm happy for all of them. There's more than enough love emanating from Dani for all three of us. But I feel... left out. Which is stupid, because it's my choice to not be standing there in front of Isaac with them.

Dani says "I do" to Nathan, then to Michael.

"Michael," she says, turning to Doc. "I love that you hear me, that you know me inside and out, and are so careful and thoughtful in how you love me. I love your smile and your heart."

"Dani." Michael stops and clears his throat. "I love you. You're my soulmate. My counterpart. The woman who understands me, who appreciates me, who supports me. I cherish every moment I've spent with you and look forward to a forever of making beautiful memories together."

I think about that word. Forever.

It's hard for me to think beyond the now. It always has been.

I've always been that guy who lived in the moment. Who existed in this practice, this game, this tournament. With one goal laid out for my future—play pro hockey and win a championship.

I always had a crush on Dani. I always hoped that someday I'd wind up with her.

But I never pictured all of this, and not because I consciously didn't want it, but because I was just enjoying the beginnings of a very fucking awesome relationship.

And yet, I'm happy they're all happy.

And I feel a little unsure how to act, how to fit in.

And I can't even have a drink because I need to stay in fighting form for the playoffs.

Michael gives Dani a soft kiss as he slides a band onto her finger. Nathan lays a deep, possessive kiss on her as he does the same.

Then Michael's cousin is pronouncing them husband and wife and husband and wife, and everyone is clapping as they turn to face the crowd, hand in hand. I give an enthusiastic, "Yeah!" as I clap, wanting them all to understand I am truly here for this. I want their happiness.

On the other side of them, Luna catches my eye, and she gives me a questioning look. I give her a grin.

When Dani and Nathan and Michael start down the aisle, I hold my arm out for my sister to take.

"You okay?" she murmurs, as we start to follow the others back down the aisle.

"I'm great. Life is good, sis."

She blows a kiss at Alexsei, Cam, and Coach Phillips as we pass them. "It sure is."

Alexsei and Owen are grinning at her, like they can't wait to put a ring on her finger, too. Cam is not grinning. I'm not sure he ever grins. But the way he looks at my sister leaves no doubt his feelings for her are just as strong as the other guys.

That's the thing. Isaac just said it—love comes in many forms.

We're all different people and we love our partners differently, both separately and together.

I want to spend the rest of my life loving Dani.

I'm going to try my best and hope like hell I don't fall short.

Because I really fucking hate it when my best isn't good enough.

CHAPTER 4
Michael

"WHO GETS to carry her over the threshold?" Crew asks. He's propped against the wall, perpendicular to where Dani is leaning against the back wall of the elevator that's taking us to the penthouse suite of the Waldorf Astoria in downtown Chicago.

Yes, we're going to a hotel room tonight. Sure, we could have gone home, but it's our wedding night. We can't jet off out of town and spend the night, or weekend, in Rome, or on a beach somewhere, or secluded in a mountain cabin because it's still hockey season. We could have waited to get married until the season was over, but…no, we couldn't.

Nathan and I would have married Dani the night she said yes to both of us. And I know our girl feels the same way. We waited long enough to put our ceremony together and for all of our loved ones to be able to get to Chicago to be with us, but that was it. We weren't waiting any longer.

So, we're stuck in the city for our wedding night and we'll have to wait on any honeymoon plans, but we can at least treat tonight as the special occasion it is and take our bride to an over-the-top hotel suite with sparkling apple juice in place of champagne, rose petals, room service, a gigantic soaker tub, and a bed that's not quite as big as the one we have at home, but will do.

"Michael should," Nathan says. He's standing in the middle of the elevator car, hands in his pants pockets, studying the lightened numbers above the elevator door, instead of looking at any of us.

I'm leaning against the back wall next to Dani. I have my hand on her lower back, stroking back and forth across the silky fabric of her dress. I can't not touch her, but I'm trying to be good. At least until we get upstairs.

She looks so damned sweet. The long, white dress, the simple make-up, the way her long hair is twisted up with just a few tendrils escaping around her face, the way her lipstick has been gone for hours, the happy sparkle in her eyes—it all combines to make her look like the perfect princess.

And I want to build her a castle and find a white horse.

I also want to tear this dress off of her and ravage her.

She's my *wife* now. That shouldn't feel as big and as different as it does, but I can't deny that hearing her proclaimed as mine out loud and in public in front of our family and friends and hearing her make vows to be mine for the rest of her life, flipped a switch inside me. I'm feeling more possessive than I ever have. The added knowledge that she's carrying a baby now has made me unable to be more than ten feet away from her. Not because I'm worried, just because when I can't see her, hear her, or touch her, I feel restless.

It's the strangest thing.

And I can read the same thing all over Nathan.

In fact, my friend, and my wife's other husband, is nearly vibrating with it.

Where I was able to socialize with friends and family tonight during the reception and force myself away from Dani, while always keeping her in sight, Nathan didn't seem able to do that. He was by her side the entire evening. He had a hand on her constantly.

Until we walked out of the reception and headed to the car to come to the hotel. He hasn't touched her once since we walked out of the building.

I think I know what's going on. At least, I hope what I think is going on is the truth.

"Why should I carry her over the threshold?" I ask. "Not that I'm not willing." I pull Dani closer and she smiles up at me. God, she's so beautiful. Always, but tonight there's an extra glow about her and it makes my heart clench just looking at her. "Just curious why I get the honor?"

Nathan still doesn't look at us. "Because once I touch her, I'm not stopping until she's wet and hot and ready and then I'm going to fuck her hard and deep and not let up until she's screaming."

Yeah, that's kind of what I suspected. He's not touching her, or even looking at her, because his resistance is hanging on by a thread.

I hear Dani's little intake of air and I see Crew shift against the wall.

"You're not going to make sweet, soft love to your beautiful bride?" Crew asks. His voice is husky.

Nathan shakes his head, still glowering at the elevator numbers that are clearly ticking upward far too slowly for his taste. "I'm going to *claim* my *wife* like a damned caveman. I've been hard as steel since she walked down that aisle looking like a gorgeous untouched virgin. She *blushed* when she looked at me and I wanted to throw her over my shoulder and take her into the next room where the whole group could hear her scream my name." He clenches his jaw. "I haven't had a minute alone with her and I'm not holding back once we get to the room."

I look down at Dani, and I see her eyes are wide and she's breathing faster. But I know she's not worried. She's excited. She doesn't seem to mind that we're talking about her in the third person. Or that the sex isn't going to be sweet and soft and romantic.

I almost chuckle. *Dani* would be making the sex dirty and hard if Nathan didn't.

Our girl is insatiable on a regular day, but I know she's just as wound up about being a wife and the love and happiness and excitement of the day. Not to mention the pregnancy hormones. I've whispered some naughty things about our wedding night in her ear and I have no doubt Nathan has done the same.

I'm not sure about Crew. He's been a little quieter and seems to be trying to stay on the perimeter today. Yes, he was part of the ceremony and he's, of course, been a part of our day. He's clearly happy and I know having him there and supportive and involved today has reassured everyone close to us that our foursome is solid. But he seems a little unsure about what exactly his place is after Best Man.

As far as I'm concerned, nothing has really changed when it comes to the four of us behind closed doors. We're still us. We still all add what we always have to our family unit.

Crew blows out a breath and looks at Dani. "Damn. You ready, pretty girl?"

She blushes at *that* too, but grins. "Very."

I see Nathan's shoulders tense, but I know it's in anticipation.

And just then, the elevator arrives on the top floor.

"Okay then," I say. I bend and sweep my wife up into my arms. "Let's go beautiful."

She loops an arm around my neck and Nathan leads us out of the elevator, with Crew following behind. I carry her over the threshold to the suite and straight to the bedroom. There's no need to pretend that isn't exactly where we all want to be.

The room is gorgeous, but I barely spare a glance at the opulent furnishings, the chandelier over the dining table, the amazing view—after all, we had all of that in Nathan's original apartment and if anyone mentions it, he'll probably bitch about how we could have just stayed there instead of moving to the brownstone.

Instead, I give us all the view we're really here for. I lay Dani on the bed in her wedding dress and step back, shrugging out of my tux jacket. "You were gorgeous today," I tell her. "You took my breath away. I can't believe that you really stood up there and promised to be mine forever. But—" I toss my jacket to the side and step to the foot of the mattress, unbuttoning my shirt cuffs and rolling a sleeve up. "I'm never letting you go now."

She gives me a smile that shoots straight through me, making my heart squeeze and my dick hard. "Good. There's nowhere I'd rather be, no other people I'd rather be with." She looks from me to Crew to Nathan. "No matter what."

Crew pulls in a deep breath, then he moves to the chair in the corner of the room. He pulls it up to the side of the bed and drops into it.

"What are you doing?" Dani asks.

"I'm going to sit back and watch my stunning, sweet, secretly-naughty-as-fuck girlfriend get fucked hard by her two new husbands," he says simply.

His eyes are dark, and he also shrugs out of his jacket and rolls his sleeves up. He looks content with being an observer. In fact, he seems very turned on by the idea.

Well, we'll see how long just watching lasts. Crew isn't very good at being left out, and Dani isn't very good about not having *everything* she wants. But we can start this way.

I look at Nathan. He's watching her with what I can only describe as a feral look in his eye.

"Should we get her out of this sweet white dress?" I ask.

Nathan shakes his head. "No." He pulls his tie loose, letting it hang around his neck as he steps to the foot of the bed. "Pull your skirt up."

Dani does as he says. Of course. She loves bossy Nathan. She gathers the full, long skirt up with both hands, gathering it until it's bunched around her waist. There's so much white fabric I wonder if she can see past it.

Nathan kneels on the floor, spreading her knees. Then he reaches up, grasps her hips and pulls her to the end of the bed.

"You've even got white panties on," he says, his voice rough.

"Yes," she says breathlessly.

"Sweet, lacy, virginal white panties that barely cover this delicious, *greedy* pussy that is anything *but* virginal," he muses. "These panties are far, far too angelic looking for what is about to happen." Then he grips the lace that rests against her hip and pulls.

The panties rip and Dani gasps. "Those were expensive, Nathan!"

He growls. "I'll buy you a hundred more. But the no-panty rule from home now applies in this suite until we check-out."

Then he leans in and gives her pussy a low, slow lick.

She moans and her head falls back.

I tuck my finger behind the bodice of her dress and drag it back and forth over the silky skin. "Does your bra match? Is it lacy and *angelic* and barely there?"

She shakes her head. "No bra."

My gaze snaps to her face. I assumed she was wearing a strapless bra or something under the dress. I kneel with one knee on the mattress next to her, sliding my finger in further and finding her hard nipple. "I'm glad I didn't know that earlier," I tell her.

"What would you have done?" she asks me, arching her back.

"Something like this." I turn my hand so I can pinch her nipple between my thumb and finger.

She sucks in a little breath, but then says, "Someone might have seen."

"Don't care," I tell her, rolling the hard tip. "You're mine. I can do whatever I want with you."

She moans. "They're more sensitive now that I'm pregnant."

I know it's the mention of her pregnancy that makes Nathan growl. He asked me the very first night if there was anything he couldn't do to or with her now that she's pregnant. I gave him the green light for anything right now. Dani is young and healthy and she's early in the pregnancy. She's a very low risk for any complications and nothing we do, even when things get a little wild, should be a problem.

He puts his face against her inner thigh. "God, you are everything," he tells her, almost worshipfully. "I love you so fucking much."

"I love yo—"

She gives a little yelp and I look down to see that Nathan has sucked and bitten her inner thigh. He loves marking her and I'm not surprised that tonight, of all nights, he feels the urge.

He licks over the mark, then licks a path up to her pussy and swipes his tongue over her clit again.

"Nathan," Dani moans.

"You need to come fast and hard, love," he tells her. "Because I need to be inside you, but I can't go slow."

She props up on her elbows so she can watch him. "Yes. God."

"And I want Michael in your ass at the same time," he tells her. "I want both of your husbands fucking you for the first time at the same time." He lifts his gaze to hers. "Say yes, Danielle."

His tone is commanding, but we all know that he absolutely wants her consent. Even though we've done this dozens of times, often because of her begging for it, we still demand her consent. It's important, and to be honest, it's hot as hell.

"Yes. God, yes," she says, nodding earnestly. She lifts her gaze to mine. "Please, Michael."

I run my hand over her hair, making myself take a deep breath. "Fuck yes."

She flops back on the bed. "*Nathan.*"

I look down to find him working her pussy like a starving man. He's got two fingers deep, his mouth latched onto her clit. He's got one hand clamped on her thigh, holding her still.

Well, I can be of some help there. I reach down and clasp both of her thighs, bringing her knees to her chest and spreading her wide for him.

She whimpers and he growls. Then his fingers thrust faster, his tongue working over her clit harder.

"Yes. Oh, my God," she moans.

"Crew!" Nathan barks suddenly, lifting his head. "Get over here."

"No way, Boss," Crew says. He's sitting back, but his hands are gripping the arms of the chair. "This is your show tonight."

"If you don't help get my wife's ass ready right now, you don't get to fuck her for a week," Nathan tells him.

It is absolutely not the threat of not fucking Dani for a week that makes Crew sit up straight. It's the treat of ass play. He fucking loves that.

And he doesn't believe the no-fucking threat anyway. That usually turns out with Crew waking Dani up in the night to fuck her right next to Nathan or Crew spreading her out on the dining room table just when Nathan walks in from work or, the one time, having her bent over Nathan's desk when he got back to this office after a meeting. All of which equally pisses the boss off and turns him on. It's always a good time when Nathan and Crew play their stupid games of chicken.

I really think this 'my wife' thing is getting to them both. It's like a taboo role-play thing. It's fucking working for me too. I have to reach down and squeeze my cock to relieve some of the ache.

"Well, hell," Crew finally says. "When you put it that way..."

"She's gotta be ready for us. You might as well be of some help," Nathan says, pushing back and straightening. He looks down at Dani. "Should we let your boyfriend get you ready?" he asks Dani. "This pretty pussy and ass are going to be filled up by your *husbands* but we can use Crew for your pleasure, right baby? You want him between your legs too?"

She nods her head, the friction against the duvet pulling more of her hair loose from her twist. "He should help. Definitely."

Nathan chuckles, hot and dark. "Even in a sweet white dress with two rings on your finger, you're still our dirty little slut, aren't you, Danielle?"

She moans and Crew swears under his breath, pushing up from the chair and stomping over to the suitcases. He digs into Nathan's, obviously trusting that the boss planned for tonight. He finds the lube. He also finds one of the little clit stimulators Dani loves.

"Okay, Mr. Armstrong, let me get your wife ready for you."

God, this is all hotter than it should be. The three of us have had Dani between us so many times this should feel routine, but it never does. Especially not tonight.

Nathan moves out of the way and then Crew's there, kneeling, running his hands up her thighs, leaning in and breathing deep.

"Oh, pretty girl, you do make a gorgeous bride," he says.

"Thank you." She ends on a moan as he licks right up her center, swirling over her clit.

"Such a dirty girl, spreading her legs for a man who's not her husband, though," he says holding the bottle of lube up so she can see him squeeze some out on his index and middle finger. "But now that I'm here—" He presses one finger against her ass and her eyes slide shut as her neck arches.

I feel her legs tense, but I hold her knees up, thighs apart. "Let him in, wife," I say softly. "I need you ready for my cock."

She lets out a long breath at that and Crew chuckles, "That's right. Don't even think about it. Just take all that pleasure. Just be the greedy girl we know you are. Spread out all wet and needing filled up." His finger sinks into her and he groans.

"Oh God," she moans.

Crew turns on the little vibrator, and with his other hand, drags it up her inner thigh. "I need you soaking and quaking and begging," he tells her. "I need your husbands to know how good I can make this so they let me keep playing."

No one in this room believes that Crew won't be a part of this every single night, but again, the roleplay is hot.

Dani tries to shift her hips on the bed, but I'm holding her still as Crew circles around her clit, not touching it with the tip of the pink vibrator.

"Crew," she pleads. "Please."

"What do you need, sweet girl?" he asks, adding a second finger to her ass and leaning in to kiss her clit.

"Yes. That. More," she pants.

"More of this?" He thrusts his fingers in and out, stretching her. "Or this?" He licks over her clit, giving her friction and pressure.

"Yes. All of it."

"What about this pretty pussy?" he asks, sliding the vibrator inside her just a half an inch.

It's not nearly big enough to really give her any relief, but the vibrations make her try to lift closer.

"More. Make me come," she begs. "Please."

"Oh, I don't know," he says. "I'm just here to help. Your husbands haven't told me that's okay."

"Michael," she says, reaching up to grasp my arm. "Let Crew make me come."

I chuckle. "I love when you beg, Cookie. I think we'll just let him edge you a little longer."

"No!" She turns to look at Nathan.

My friend is clearly barely holding it together.

"Nathan," she pleads. "I need to come."

"Oh, I know you do." He looks pleased by that. He smooths his hand over her hair. "But not yet."

"Please!" Crew touches the vibrator to her clit and she gasps. "Yes! More!"

He leaves it there a little longer, pumping his fingers into her ass, but as she's climbing, her grip on my arm tightening, he suddenly removes the vibrations.

Her body slumps. "Crew!" she protests.

"But we're just getting started," he tells her. "You don't want the fun over too quickly, do you?"

He moves the vibrator to her pussy again, sliding it deep, fucking her for a few thrusts, and again, just as she's climbing, removes it.

"Please," she whimpers. "Let me come. You know I will again."

We all chuckle at that. We do know that. Dani has no trouble having multiple orgasms.

Now Crew moves the vibrator to her ass, sliding it in easily as it's smaller than his two fingers together. Her moan is much louder now. "I need something in my pussy. *Please*."

"This is so fun though," Nathan tells her. He combs his fingers through her tresses, the deep red of her hair gorgeous against the white bedspread. "God, I love seeing you panting and needy."

"I am." She grabs his arm. "I need you."

His eyes narrow. He's been on edge all day and we all know that Dani could easily push him over.

"Take her dress off," he finally says.

I'm not sure who he's talking to, but I'm the one who moves. I lift her up, slide the zipper down, and strip the mounds of white material over her head, tossing it onto the floor.

Then our bride is bare naked, laid out for us, needy and hot and wet—just the way we like her.

"Crew?" Nathan asks, staring down at Dani.

"Yeah, Boss?" His voice is tight.

"Would you like to come all over our wife?"

"Jesus," Crew mutters. "Yeah, I fucking would."

"Do it. Cover her."

Crew gets to his feet. He tosses the vibrator on the floor. "I want her to come with me."

Fair enough. I reach down, slide three fingers into Dani's hot, wet pussy, and press my thumb to her clit.

Crew lowers his pants and takes his cock out, eyes on Dani the whole time. She's moaning and pressing up against my hand, but says, "Take your shirt off."

Crew simply lifts his hands to the front of his shirt and rips it open, the buttons flying. Then, chest and abs on display for Dani, he fists his cock, stroking hard and fast. "I want my name on your lips this time," he tells her. "While your husbands watch. You can scream their names later while they fuck you, but I want you with *me* right now."

She's breathing fast and I can feel her pussy clutching my fingers already. "*Yes*."

Crew's hand is moving fast and rough over his cock and he

climbs up on the bed next to her. "Come with me, Dani," he says gruffly.

"Crew," she moans.

"Come on, pretty girl." His jaw is tight. "Come on."

Then she's there, her pussy squeezing me, her head thrown back, crying out, "*Crew*!"

"Fuck yes," he grits out as he starts to come. Ribbons of white shoot out over her stomach and tits. "Fuck. *Dani*."

As soon as he's finished, or possibly just before he's totally done, Nathan is pulling her off the end of the bed, wrapping his arms around her and then lying back where she just was. He stripped sometime between Crew climbing up on the bed and now.

"Ride me," he tells her.

Dani seems slightly dazed, endorphins likely coursing, but she pushes herself up, straddling his thighs.

He smacks her ass. "You're ready. Take my cock right now."

She reaches down, takes his cock in hand, then lowers herself over him. They both groan and Nathan grips her hips tightly, just holding her still for a moment, as if needing to gather himself.

"Hughes. Now." That's all he says.

I think maybe that's all he's able to say.

I move to the end of the bed and shrug out of my shirt. I smooth my hand up and down Dani's back, marveling as always how soft and silky her skin is and how fucking gorgeous she can look with another man's cock inside her. "Fuck, Dani," I say softly. "You're so beautiful like this. You ready?"

"So, so ready," she says.

I run my hand over her ass, then test her with first one finger, then a second. She presses back against me, clearly wanting more. I grab the lube, get us both ready, then get in position and press against her.

"This is it, Danielle," Nathan tells her. "Your wifely duties begin. You sure you can handle this?"

"I'm exactly the woman to handle this," she says, her eyes on his. "To handle *you*, and all of you, together."

God, I love how her confidence has blossomed. She's exactly the sweet, loving woman we all fell in love with months ago, but she's becoming more and more sure of herself and how she's the glue in this whole relationship. It's fucking sexy as hell to see her find her power.

Nathan shudders and clasps the back of her neck, pulling her down into a deep kiss as I reach around, cup one breast, teasing the nipple, and ease my cock into her.

Our three deep moans fill the room. Crew has collapsed in the chair again. His body seems relaxed, but he's watching Dani raptly, his expression full of desire and love.

I grip her hips. "Okay, my girl, here we go," I tell her tightly. I move out a few inches, then back in.

She pulls her mouth from Nathan's to gasp my name.

I pull out and thrust in again. The feel of her tight around me is heaven and hell. I could easily lose it in two more thrusts. Part of me wants to grab her hair, pull her head back, and slam into her.

Making her my wife hasn't made this all feel sweeter. At least not at the moment. I want to *claim* her. I want to fuck her even harder. It's crazy.

"Yes, Michael. Harder," my sweet, amazing greedy girl encourages.

Fuck. I grit my teeth and pick up my pace a bit.

Nathan is fucking her pussy deep and hard as well, but Dani is taking every stroke. She's so amazing.

"Such a good girl," I praise, stroking my hand down her back. "Taking us both, taking us so deep. You need all of this, don't you?"

"Yes. God, *yes*," she breathes. She reaches back and grasps my arm. "I feel like I can never get enough of you. Even when you're all filling me up—"

She breaks off as Nathan thrusts even harder.

Her moan is so beautiful. Her inner muscles tighten around us, and I see goosebumps break out over her skin.

Fuck it. I reach up and wrap her gorgeous hair around my hand, making a fist. I pull, tipping her head back. It causes her body to arch, and Nathan immediately lifts a hand to start plucking and pinching her nipples.

A shiver of pleasure goes through her.

I put my mouth to her ear. "Think of all those sweet, virginal brides who go to bed with their nice, respectable husbands on their wedding nights, just the two of them, and have sex in missionary with the lights off?" I kiss her neck, her shoulder, scraping my teeth over the skin. "Those poor girls. They have no idea how deep they can be filled up, how much their pussies can take, how it would feel to be *worshiped* by three men who want to make them come more than they want to take their next breath."

"*Michael*," she practically whimpers.

"But you know, don't you Dani?" I ask, dragging my beard along her neck. "You know how fucking amazing it is to be wanton, to turn your body over to three men who love you so damned much that making you come is their sole purpose. You know how it feels to make three grown men absolute idiots for you. You know how it feels to have all the power over three men who thought they had everything figured out, knew who they were, what they wanted, and how everything was going to play out until you came along and turned everything upside down."

Nathan and I are thrusting deep, hard, in a rhythm that is taking her slowly, but steadily, toward the pinnacle.

"You know exactly what a gorgeous, sweet little witch you are and that we'd do anything for you." I squeeze her ass. "Tell us that you know. Tell us that you know you have all the power."

She gasps and shakes her head. "I… can't… think."

Nathan's hand is on her ass now, and he gives her a smack. "Say it, Danielle. Tell us you know your power."

She shakes her head again, but then swivels her hips, and Nathan swears as I groan.

"Vixen." Nathan smacks her ass again. "You know you're in charge."

She doesn't say anything, but she does the hip thing again.

I clamp down on her hips, holding her still. "You're in charge even when you're full of two cocks, Danielle. Jesus, you beautiful wicked little thing."

"I have the power," she says, breathlessly. "God, I *love* that you're all mine and that you'll do all of the amazing dirty things to me that I need."

"Everything we have is yours," Nathan tells her, his voice tight.

She takes a deep breath. "Then *fuck me hard*. Spank me. Make me come. *Please*."

Nathan growls and lifts his head to take her nipple in his mouth.

I spank her again, harder this time.

And we both pick up our pace again, fucking her fast and hard.

Moments later she tightens around us and cries out. "Yes, yes!"

I'm right there, emptying into her. Nathan roars out his orgasm seconds later, holding onto her right above my hands, filling her up.

The room fills with only the sound of us breathing hard.

Dani slumps forward onto Nathan's chest.

I take several deep breaths, smoothing my hands over her back, before pulling out. I lean over and kiss her shoulder, then head into the bathroom to clean up.

When I get back, Crew has already scooped her up off of Nathan and is holding her, wrapped in a sheet, in his lap in the chair as Nathan heads for the bathroom next.

I take her from Crew, clean her up with the washcloth I brought with me, then I tuck her into the bed.

Crew strips and climbs in next to her, but when Nathan and I both return to the room, Crew's left room right next to Dani for me.

Nathan always gets her right side, but Crew and I share her left side.

Tonight Crew's letting me cuddle up next to my new wife.

"Thanks," I tell him softly as he reaches to turn off the light.

"Of course," he says easily. "Where you belong tonight." His voice is sleepy, but he sounds content.

I settle onto my pillow, next to my wife on our wedding night, with her other husband and her boyfriend like bookends on either side of us.

And it all feels pretty damned perfect.

CHAPTER 5
Sammy the Malamute
(WADE)

WHEN I STARE up at the giant scoreboard, I see the clock counting down in what feels like slow motion. Ten, nine, eight seconds left in the championship game. The Racketeers are tied with the Beavers 1-1 in what has been a boring game of defense. Or I'm just hot and a little high in my Sammy costume.

Maybe more than a little high.

I might actually be tripping balls.

But I can't help it.

Watching Luna McNeill hang all over what's-his-whatever in the stands while I'm just the guy in the dog suit has me, like, heartbroken. Devastated. I'm Lady without the Tramp.

Wait. That's wrong. I would be Tramp. Right?

Fuck, I don't even know now.

I just know it sucks because she's probably my soulmate and now I'll be destined to wander this planet alone for all of eternity.

Or I might have taken too many edibles.

I lean over the railing at the top of the stairs where I'm not blocking anyone's view and try to focus on where the puck is.

There. That magical little disc of hockey happiness is floating across the ice, massaged by a stick. Left, right, left. I'm transfixed.

I glance up at the clock.

Four, three, two seconds.

He shoots. There's a collective gasp from the fans. He scores.

It takes me until the buzzer to realize it's the other team who just got the puck past Racketeers goalie Wilder.

Well, holy shit, that's like *bad*. The Racketeers have lost the championship.

Blake Wilder is now lying face down on the ice, pounding it with his giant glove. He gives a roar of anger and agony.

Crew McNeill skates over to him and bends down to murmur something to him. The rest of the Racketeers players have their heads hanging down in disappointment.

The Beavers are in a pile-on on the guy who scored the goal, sticks raised in triumph.

The arena is deathly silent, and I slowly turn to see Luna has her hand over her mouth in horror.

Dani, Mr. Armstrong's wife, has tears running down her face.

The big man looks pissed. I start to back up and away, so I'm not on his radar.

Some smart dude once said there's always next year, but that dude never met the owner of the Racketeers.

Mr. Armstrong can be fucking scary.

CHAPTER 6
Crew

WE LOST.

I can't believe we fucking lost.

This wasn't supposed to happen.

I was supposed to make the *opposite* happen.

And we fucking lost.

It's all my fault. Of course, everyone is reassuring me that's not the case. It was a team effort. Other people made mistakes too. Sure, but I'm the scorer for the team. The hotshot. That's what I'm there for.

I didn't score at all in our last game. In fact, I missed three shots. Sure, one would've been a miracle shot, but I should not have missed the other two.

I look down at the beer in front of me. I haven't been able to drink in weeks. Tonight, of all nights, I should want to get shitfaced. But the beer tastes like shit. The music sounds like shit. Everything is shit.

And then worse, one of my favorite teammates and friends is a fucking eternal sunshine, and he chose the seat right across the table from me.

"Well, I've got to say, going home at the end of this season feels a lot better than it has for the past couple, right

McNeill?" Alexsei Ryan has the audacity to actually grin at me.

Grin.

The night after the biggest loss of my career.

I scowl at him. I'm not in the fucking mood.

The coaches thought it was a good idea for us to come out and socialize tonight. And to show the fans and media that we're out, coming together as a team, brushing off the loss and still celebrating our amazing season.

Fuck that.

Yeah, we had a hell of a season. We had a hell of a playoff season too. We should be proud.

Yeah, yeah. I hear it all. And even agree with it somewhere deep down. But I wanted it all. And it was *right there.*

I haven't talked about it with anyone.

We made rules at home a long time ago about this. When we're at home, we're not Racketeers. We're Crew, Nathan, and Michael. Not the star player, the team owner, and the team doctor.

But...*fuck.*

It's pretty hard to avoid the fact that Nathan is my damned boss.

And I let him down last night.

Armstrong drafted me because the chances for a championship went up exponentially with me on the roster.

And it absolutely looked like I was worth every fucking penny.

Until last night.

It would make it really hard to face my boss the next day anyway, but it's worse when I'm seeing him in my kitchen—that's actually *our* kitchen. Or when I want to just wallow on my couch —that I also know he hates. Or when I want to fuck out my frustrations with my girlfriend, or even just cuddle with her and have her remind me that everything will be okay, but he's in the same damned bed.

Not to mention that girl who's supposed to kiss it all better, is his *wife*.

Yeah, you can say things at home are a little complicated.

"Take your sunshine and rainbow shitting unicorns somewhere else," I tell Alexsei. "It's too soon."

I have been labeled as the sunshine in our relationship at home, but I've got nothing on Alexsei Ryan. The guy was born with glitter in his veins, I swear. He can be happy within thirty seconds of shit going down.

To make matters even worse, he's madly in love now. And not with just one person. He's now got his longtime friend turned lover, Cam *and* the girl Alexsei had crushed on for months and that he now shares with his boyfriend, in his bed every night.

The girl who happens to be my sister.

I probably should've stayed home. Or gone pretty much *anywhere* else.

"Fine, be miserable. There's nothing we can do to change it now," Alexsei tells me. "We just need to come back stronger next year. It's not the end of the world, man. You have a gorgeous girl at home, and now some time off to enjoy her. Life is good if you really think about it. Hockey will be there in a few months and we'll have another chance."

Sure. If I 'really think about it', the girl I'm supposed to be spending time with is spending her free time planning her honeymoons. Yes, *honeymoons*, plural, because of course Armstrong can't share *that*. So it's not like she'll be around for the entire off season for me to enjoy all on my own.

I never feel jealous of Michael and Nathan. So this new emotion isn't helping me at all. In fact, it's making me even grumpier. I don't want to be jealous of them. And I'm very aware of the fact that I could easily be planning a honeymoon with Dani, too. It's my choice that I'm not.

Basically, I'm just miserable all the way around.

"I am ready to make you feel all better." A feminine voice catches my attention, and I lift my gaze to find my sister wrapping her arms around Alexsei and pressing a kiss to his neck.

One of his big beefy arms goes around her and he pulls her up close, gripping her chin and turning her mouth to his for a deep, hot kiss.

And there's one more thing on my list of just-kill-me-now things.

I don't hate that they're together. I love them both, and they are very happy, not just together, but with Cam, and Coach Phillips, my sister's *other* boyfriend. Yeah, apparently this poly thing runs in my family.

I don't mind that my sister is dating a teammate and friend, but I don't necessarily need it thrown in my face when I'm trying to wallow in my misery. And I certainly don't need to think about how she might be working to cheer him up.

"Hey goddess," Alexsei greets. "You smell like sugar." He nuzzles her neck.

"Bet you taste like it, too."

My sister, barely sparing me a glance, giggles. Luna McNeill giggling is probably the most stunning thing of all. "Cam said I did," she tells Alexsei.

He growls. "I've been down here being a good teammate, nursing my wounds, and you've been at home letting my boyfriend *taste* you?"

"Well, define 'let'." She gives him a sassy grin.

Alexsei's hand drops to her ass. "Am I going to have to have a talk with him?"

"If you do, you'll have to talk to Owen, too," she says. "He was the one holding me down."

I slap my hand down on the top of the table. "I am probably the coolest brother anyone has ever had but I'm drawing a line there. Knock it off."

Luna laughs, but Alexsei is still frowning at her. "So Coach is feeling pretty good about our loss, then?"

She shrugs. "It was his idea. Cam and I asked him what would make him feel better." She shoots me a glance. "I could tell you in graphic detail how he explained it to us, but maybe we should go somewhere we can be alone."

Alexsei immediately stands from his stool. He tosses some bills on the table and says, "See you later, McNeill," then he's dragging my sister out of the bar.

I shake my head and try to be grateful that at least she didn't launch into those details with me sitting here.

I feel a hard slap on my back and look up as Blake Wilder, our goalie, joins me at the table. "You okay, man?"

I shake my head. "Not at all. You?"

I know he's been beating himself up almost as much as I have. The winning goal for the Beavers slid past him after all. But it was my fault that it came down to a tied game where that one goal made all the difference.

"Feeling pretty shitty, to be honest."

Jack Hayes takes the seat next to him and reaches over to set another bottle of the beer I was drinking in front of me.

"It sucks," Jack agrees.

I welcome their company more than Alexsei's.

I love Ryan but *this* is the energy I want right now.

I want fellow players to mope with.

"Can't believe it came down to the last second," Jack says, shaking his head. "I've been replaying the game in my mind for the past twenty-four hours. It just sucks."

I nod. "Can't even be upset about any calls. Can't really point any fingers. Everybody played their hearts out."

Blake points a big, thick finger at me. "Including you."

I don't make eye contact. I just lift my beer. "Yeah."

Wilder leans in, resting his huge forearms on the table. "Look, he probably wasn't supposed to say anything. And I know I'm sure as hell not supposed to tell you what he said," the big man says.

I tense and look up.

"But Doc said that you're taking it really hard." Blake shakes his head. "You can't man. It's not only on you."

Fucking Michael. Michael's insight is awesome sometimes. And annoying as fuck other times. I'm not surprised he knows I'm blaming myself, but I was hoping the fact that he hadn't pressed any deep conversations at home meant that he was going to let me just deal with it on my own.

I should've known better.

I also know that when I am ready to talk, if I need any advice or just to rant, Michael will be there for me.

None of us have talked about the game, hockey, or the Racketeers at home at all. We haven't even talked about not talking about it. Last night after the loss, Dani simply met me at the door, wrapped her arms around me, and I carried her up to the bedroom, undressed us both and just held her. Nathan and Michael just left us alone, not coming to bed until after I was asleep. This morning Michael made breakfast like always and he and Nathan both went into the arena as usual.

Since I didn't have any injuries to have the medical team check on, I stayed home. Dani and I snuggled and played video games and ordered food in for lunch.

I didn't see Nathan or Michael before leaving to come join the guys down here tonight.

But we'll probably have to talk it out, eventually. Hockey is a huge part of my life. Obviously, Nathan and Michael's as well. The Racketeers is what brought us all together. And eventually I am going to have to apologize to Nathan.

I know that Nathan is pissed. I also know that he's not specifically pissed at me. I mean, maybe a little. I didn't play a perfect game. But Nathan doesn't blame me for the loss. I know that. At the same time, I know the game was more than just a game. It was more than just his team losing.

Nathan wanted the championship for his grandfather, the previous Racketeers owner.

Stanford has Alzheimer's, and is slowly but surely fading away. Nathan wanted this championship to happen while his grandfather was still aware enough to enjoy it.

I feel tears stinging the back of my eyes.

Fuck. That's part of why this is bothering me so much, too.

Because of Nathan and our relationship, I've gotten to know Stanford personally. I wanted this championship for him almost as much as Nathan did. Who knows how Stanford will be in a year? If we win next year, will he know? Will he understand and be able to enjoy it?

I scrub a hand over my face.

This family and relationship thing has definitely complicated my life.

If I hadn't met Dani and gotten involved with the guys, I would be pissed tonight, I would be down, and I would be feeling like I failed my team.

But now I have *more* people in my life who I can fail. More people to let down. More people to care about.

Most days I love that.

Today is not one of those days.

"I'm sorry I couldn't pull it out for us," I finally say to Blake and Jack. I haven't apologized to anyone yet and it feels good to say the words *I'm sorry*.

They both scowl at me as expected. "It's not just your fucking fault," Jack says. "This team is not entirely your responsibility, McNeill."

"I know. But I don't feel like I did my part."

And as I say those words out loud, I feel an aching in my chest.

That's it. It's not that I felt like I had to do it all, but I do feel like I didn't do what everyone was depending on me to do.

And I fucking feel that way at home too.

It hits me between the eyes. I've felt restless ever since the guys proposed to Dani.

We had the heart to heart. I believe that they all understand where I'm at and are supportive. I'm not afraid of losing Dani exactly.

But I can't shake this feeling that I'm not doing my part. The pie at home should be divided into four equal parts.

Right now, that's not true. My slice is much smaller.

And that's my choice.

Just then, a gorgeous, curvy, brunette slides up between Jack and Blake.

I know Elise. She works in my sister's bakery. She's bold, sassy, and hilarious. She's also, apparently, just recently discovered she has a love for hockey.

Well, hockey players anyway.

"So there are three really cute young girls over at the bar who are wondering if you two need some comforting." She meets my gaze. "They know all about you. Not to say they didn't express their disappointment that you're already taken."

I love that all of Chicago knows about my relationship. And that they're mostly supportive. That does add a little warmth to the cold rock that seems to be resting in my chest.

Blake turns partially on his stool. "Which ones?" he asks.

"Two blondes and the brunette at the end of the bar. They've all got margaritas." Elise says the word 'margaritas' with clear derision.

Elise definitely strikes me as the shoot–straight–tequila type of girl.

Blake shakes his head and turns back around. "Nah."

Jack lifts his drink to his lips and takes a draw. "Nope. Not me either."

Elise looks between them with eyebrows arched. "What's wrong with you? They're gorgeous and willing."

"Way too small for me," Blake says. "I like women, not girls. And they need to have some curves. Something to really hold on to."

As he says this, his gaze tracks over Elise from head to toe.

Rather than blushing, or acting flustered in the slightest, Elise cocks one hip and plants her hand on it. "Is that right? I suppose you think you should just get your pick of any woman anywhere?"

Blake drags his tongue over his bottom lip and then turns back to the table. "Seems to work that way."

Elise laughs. She doesn't roll her eyes, doesn't call him on his bullshit, she just laughs as if his ego genuinely delights her.

Jack grins widely. "I mean, it definitely helps the rest of us that Crew and Alexsei are off the market."

She laughs again and then leans in closer to Jack. "Now see, I believe everything that Wilder just said. But I don't believe *that* coming out of your mouth."

He tips his head. "Coming from you, that's a compliment."

"How's that?" she asks.

"Spoken as someone who knows very well that she can have anybody in this bar. Male or female, probably."

She gives him a smirk and then scans the room. "Good to know. Thank you."

"Yeah, well, don't forget this table is in this room," he says.

She chuckles softly, then reaches up and pats his cheek. "You're so cute."

She acts as if she's about to move off when Blake reaches out and grasps her wrist. She turns back.

"You don't think I'm cute?" he asks.

Now her gaze rakes over him from head to toe. She shakes her head. "Cute? No."

Then she shakes off his grasp, turns, and saunters back across the bar.

I watch as both Wilder and Hayes watch every swing of her hips.

"Your tongues are practically on the table, guys."

Jack shakes his head, his attention still across the bar. "I know."

Blake takes a breath and then blows it out. "I can't believe she thought that I was even going to notice those other three girls as long as she's in this room."

"You have a thing for Elise?" I ask.

"Well, I'm not dead, stupid, or married," he says. "So, yeah."

I chuckle and have to admit that watching this little flirtation has definitely cheered me up a little.

"Well, Elise is a bit of a handful. You sure?"

Blake gives me a grin. "Well, I guess it's good I've got two big hands then."

By the time Andrew, the driver who works for Nathan, but now is essentially our family's driver, drops me off in front of the brownstone, I'm feeling a little better.

Less pissy, less sad, and now more just disappointed.

In the outcome of the game.

In my performance.

In myself, in general.

The game and the loss sucked.

The fact that my girlfriend is going to be jetting off on her honeymoon with another man sucks.

The fact that right after she gets home from that trip, she's going to be leaving with her other husband on her second honeymoon also sucks.

But I realize as I stand in front of our brownstone, looking up at the house that we bought, renovated, and moved into together with high hopes for the future, I don't have it so bad.

This is home. I feel happy, comforted, and safe here.

The three people inside are the most important people in my life.

And I still get to play hockey.

Sure, my boss might be pissed at me, but he did still replace my cereal and my Gatorade when he placed our grocery order yesterday.

I figure he can't be too mad if he's still buying me Fruity Loopies *and* Peanut Butter Coco Balls.

Yes, he did get the generic brand ones with no toys inside, but that's a Nathan thing to do, not a Mr. Armstrong thing to do.

CHAPTER 7
Dani

"THANKS, AUSTIN. HAVE A GOOD NIGHT." I wave as our bookshop employee heads to the front door at the end of his shift.

Austin gives me a cheerful wave back before exiting.

He helped run another successful book club tonight, this one for mystery and thriller lovers. Since the previous fall, our attendance at these events has been steadily growing and we now have book clubs for varying genres and nonfiction interest groups twice a week. It's been exciting to see an explosion of interest in reading in our community, and we've hosted two author signings now as well.

I suspect one or two of the dedicated attendees are just hoping for a sighting of a certain professional hockey player, but they're destined to be disappointed. Crew hasn't been around Books and Buns for months given his training and practice schedule with the playoffs and the championship. Now that the season is sadly over, he's mostly been brooding in his hot tub or hanging out in his game room in the basement of our house. It's a little concerning but both Michael and Nathan have assured me he just needs his space to recover from the disappointment of losing the championship.

I rise up slowly from my chair and take a deep breath. I'm

tired all the time these days and I need to have a serious conversation with Luna about the future of our shared business venture. We both love our respective sides of Books and Buns, and what we've created together, but I don't know how much time I have to dedicate to it right now, especially now that both sides of the store are booming.

Luna is in the bakery, helping Lydia remove all the remaining pastries to put in the fridge for the night since we're closing in a couple of minutes. I'm so proud of what she's done with the bakery. Everything she bakes looks, smells, and tastes amazing.

"Can I have a pain au chocolat before you put those away?" I ask as I approach the counter.

"Of course. No more morning sickness?" Luna uses tongs to grab a bun and put it on a plate for me.

"It's definitely better. Now I'm craving sugar nonstop. Michael says it's something to do with my body self-regulating insulin levels since I wasn't eating much and deficiencies in something or other because of the pregnancy."

"You are growing a human from nothing," Luna says cheerfully.

The thought has me feeling warm inside and out.

I still can't quite believe we're having a baby. The reality of that hasn't fully sunk in yet.

"He says I need to eat more protein but this pastry seems way more appealing than grilled chicken."

"Amen to that." Luna grins.

Lydia reemerges from the kitchen. "How was book club?" she asks me.

She's been working primarily for Luna since before Christmas and she's in high school. She also happens to be dating Owen Phillips' son, Brady, which has been adorable to watch. Brady looks at Lydia like she's the most beautiful girl in Chicago and I love seeing that.

"It was great. We had a nice mix of attendees tonight.

Murder and crime isn't really my thing, but Austin enjoys hosting and he's good at guiding the readers through questions."

I'm leaning on the counter and I grab a fork and knife to cut my pastry.

"Hmm, that's interesting because I seem to remember that you were writing an online serial about mafia dudes and stolen brides and murder not too long ago."

I glance up to see Luna giving me an indulgent smile.

She's right, of course. It took Michael suggesting that I write rom coms to realize that I was trying to fit my style of writing into a popular genre.

"Speaking of Habanero..." Luna has inadvertently given me the opening I need to have this conversation. "My new story has really taken off on it."

The serial reading app has been so much fun for me and I've found a lot of success on it with my latest work.

"I know. Crew told me. My best friend didn't tell me because she's too busy being married, but my brother told me all about it." Luna doesn't look or sound annoyed. She's just loading pastries onto a tray.

Lydia disappears back into the kitchen with the loaded tray.

"And being pregnant," Luna adds in a stage whisper with a wink. "Can you guys please tell everyone soon? It's literally killing me to keep it quiet. I did tell Owen though. I'm sorry, I couldn't stop myself."

She doesn't even really sound sorry. It makes me laugh. "Luna! What if he says something to Crew? Then you and I will both be in trouble."

"He won't. Owen is a steel trap. Just be thankful I didn't tell Alexsei. He can't keep a secret to save his life."

"Well, I would love to tell everyone. The plan is to officially tell our parents next week after the first doctor's appointment. After that, we'll make some kind of announcement and you won't have to keep it a secret anymore."

"Thank God. Your boobs are already getting huge. There won't be any explaining that in another week or two."

That makes me laugh. "Right? I already need new bras. It's crazy."

Lydia has returned from the kitchen but she goes to the front door to lock it and starts wiping down the tables in the bakery.

"So, anyway, my new story…" I lick the tip of the fork, a little giddy over the news I want to share. "I was contacted yesterday by a major publishing house in New York. They want to publish my serial story as a romance novel."

"*What?*" Luna pauses in her cleaning and stands straight up, her hands on her hips. "Are you freaking kidding me? Dani, that's awesome! I'm so proud of you!"

"I'm so proud of you, too," I tell her truthfully. "You've made this business take off, with very little help from me." I don't pause, not wanting to give her time to say otherwise. I know it's true. I've been wrapped up in my relationship with all the guys. "And I want you to know that moving forward, I feel like the decisions about the bookstore need to be more yours than mine." I rush ahead. "If you want to close it or expand the bakery or whatever you want, it's fine with me. I just don't think that I can—

Luna holds her hand up. "Whoa. Just slow down for a second. Let's just back that up and take a minute to enjoy how fucking amazing it is that a publisher wants to make a *book* out of your story. That is incredible. We need to just pause and celebrate that. I mean, you're going to say yes, right?"

I nod enthusiastically. "Oh, yes, absolutely. Nathan had his lawyer look at the offer and it's solid for a debut author. They're paying me and everything." I still honestly can't believe that. "It's a dream come true."

"I'm so happy for you. And this is perfect for you, with the baby coming and everything. You can write when you can or when the muse strikes or the baby is napping or the guys are out of town. It's a perfect career for you at this point in your life."

I breathe a sigh of relief. I knew Luna would be happy for me but I have been worried for a while now that she would be upset with me for pulling back from the business. "I knew you would understand. I love the creative outlet, and feeling like I have something just for me, but my life has changed dramatically. I have three guys who want my attention and a baby on the way who is going to be demanding of my time and energy. I just don't know that I'll have time to be at the bookstore much anymore."

Luna nods slowly, fingering the crescent moon necklace she wears frequently. "I get it. I don't think I'll make any decisions right away. I'm not sure the bakery needs an expansion, and the bookstore is holding its own right now. Maybe I can just hire someone to be a full-time manager on that side. Maybe Austin would be interested or I can find someone else to work with him."

I'm grateful she's being so understanding. I still feel guilty, though. "I can help you hire someone, or talk to Austin. I don't want to leave you in a lurch." I shove a bite of pastry into my mouth so I don't talk myself back out of stepping away from the business. I know I can't handle it and a baby as well.

"No worries. We'll work it out. It's not like you can bring a baby to work."

"I mean, I could. I'm sure people do it, but I want to give the baby my full attention." I brush my hand over my stomach. I have the tiniest little bulge that no one but me and my guys would ever notice.

It's been incredible to watch them studying my changing body with varying expressions, from feral possessiveness to tender awe and joy that we've created a baby together.

"Oh, please. Nathan would never let you work, let's be honest." Luna grins. "He's going to have you sitting on silk pillows for the first three months."

"He can be a little over-the-top," I admit. "He's already talking about getting us on a waitlist for the best preschool in Chicago."

"A waitlist? Please. Nathan will just donate a million dollars to whatever school you want this baby to go to and you'll have a spot."

She's one hundred percent right. "It's really sweet to see how much he wants this baby." I sigh, as happy as I've ever been. "Too bad I can't say the same for your brother."

"Is Crew being an asshole? I warned you about him," she tells me.

"Of course he's not being an asshole." I feel the need to defend him. "He's just nervous."

"Well, that's normal. Aren't you nervous? I would be freaking out."

"I'm more nervous than I want to admit. This is a huge life change. An amazing one, but I haven't even babysat since I was fifteen. So yes, I'm nervous. But Crew, I don't know. I feel like I don't really know what's going on in his head right now."

"He's upset about losing the championship. It probably doesn't have anything to do with the baby. Alexsei was a little pouty right after the game, and he's never pouty. But," Luna adds. "This was really big for Crew. He put everything into bringing that championship to our hometown in his first season. It's like he wanted to prove to everyone that bringing him here was the right move."

"It was the right move," I say quickly. "Everyone thinks so."

"I know that. But Crew might not be feeling it right now."

"You're right." I need to be more sensitive to what Crew is going through right now. His dream was shattered in those final seconds. "At least none of us are dating Blake Wilder," I say, shaking my head. "He must be a nightmare right now to be around."

"Never date a goalie," Luna declares. "It's a hockey rule."

"I'm not sure I like that rule," Elise says, popping out from the kitchen as she pulls her apron off over her head. "I love me a beefy goalie."

"Don't do it. Their bad day is like a *really fucking bad* day." Luna gestures to me. "Guess what, though? Dani is going to be a published romance author! She got offered a publishing deal."

"Shut up! That's fantastic. Congrats!"

"Thank you." I put my hands to my cheeks, pausing briefly to admire my wedding bands on my ring finger. "Holy crap, is this my real life? Two incredible husbands, one amazing boyfriend, plus a book deal?"

And a baby.

Cookie & Co. is adding a little nugget and I feel like the luckiest woman on the planet.

CHAPTER 8
Crew

"DANIELLE IS UPSTAIRS WRITING. I'm heading out. It might be late."

I tip my head back against the couch cushion to look at Nathan as he shrugs into his jacket.

He's on his way out to some big fancy dinner with some new potential sponsors.

Michael's already out. He's over at Garrett and Deb's house, helping put together some crazy bookcase system in their home library.

Of course Michael has friends who have a home library.

Even though Dani and I are both welcome at the sponsor's dinner and at the Baker's house, we opted for a night in, just the two of us. Dani's been getting tired earlier in the night as her pregnancy progresses and both of these events had the potential to stretch past her bedtime.

I'm very much looking forward to having her to myself. It feels like we haven't had a lot of one-on-one time in the past few weeks. Between the end of the season, the wedding, and baby stuff, it feels like everything has been a tornado of emotion and activity.

"Sounds good," I tell Nathan. "See you later."

We've been speaking, but Nathan and I haven't spent any time alone either.

He pauses by the front door, then looks over at me. "Can we talk for a minute?"

I frown and sit up a little straighter. "Is everything okay?" My first thoughts go to Dani. And the baby, of course. She had a doctor's appointment the other day. It was the first. Michael insisted that it was routine, and we didn't all need to be there. In fact, he thought it would be overwhelming for the doctor and staff to have the four of us crowded into a tiny exam room. Luna had offered to go with Dani instead, but Nathan had insisted on being the one to accompany her.

They'd come home and told us everything was great, though. They've been all smiles and glowing faces and renewed excitement now that everything was official and there was a medical chart.

"It's not about Danielle," Nathan says, clearly reading me. "I think you and I need to talk about…us."

Ugh. That should sound weird. But that just means it's about hockey. The subject we've been avoiding because we have a rule about that at home and I've been avoiding the arena.

I sigh. "Fine. I can come by your office tomorrow." I guess I can't put it off forever.

But Nathan shakes his head. "Just come outside."

I lift a brow. "Literally just outside the house counts as complying to the no-hockey-talk-at-home rule?"

He shrugs. "Why not?" Which not only confirms that this conversation will be about hockey, the Racketeers, and the championship, but means he doesn't want to put it off.

Dammit.

I push up from the couch. Might as well get it over with.

I follow him out the front door and down the steps. He doesn't stop until he's out on the sidewalk, the first strip of public property.

I chuckle, but then when he stops and turns to face me, I

swallow hard. I have something I need to say to him, too, and it's probably past due.

"I'm sorry," I say before he can speak. I tuck my hands into the pockets of my athletic shorts. "I let you down, and I feel like shit. But I promise you, my head and heart are here and next season I'm gonna give it my all."

Nathan nods, then says, "That's what I want to talk about."

I frown and my heart rate picks up, even though I know the chances that Nathan is going to cut me from the team or trade me away are almost zero. Even if I wasn't his wife's boyfriend–which still sounds fucking weird. We lost our final game, but I had a hell of a season.

I decide to point that out. "I played my ass off for you this year," I say. "This is where I want to be. Please tell me you're not doubting my dedication. I have a lot of good hockey years ahead, and I want to spend them here in Chicago."

He frowns. "Good. I didn't realize any of that was in question."

I frown back at him. "Well I didn't think it was either, but the way you're acting--"

"I'm acting like a guy who really cares about someone who cares about hockey more than anything else in his life and took the loss really hard. I'm talking to you as a friend. Hell as more than a friend. We're...whatever we are. It's tense at home and part of that's on me. But I'm not standing here talking to you as your owner." He pauses. "I'm sorry you thought that. We need to figure out how to be both things...all of the things...we are to each other. I think that's just going to take us some more time."

I let that sink in and then straighten. "Oh." I pause, swallow, then say, "Thank you. But," I add quickly. "I don't care about hockey more than anything else. It's not my only love anymore. But I hope that you, of all people, are glad to hear that and understand."

Nathan nods. "Of course I am. But..." He shoves a hand through his hair. "Fuck, McNeill, I don't care about hockey more than anything else either. Anymore. And yes, that means Danielle, but it also means you. A year ago, yes, you were only a player to me and how you performed on the ice was key. Now...of course, it's more than that. I'll be honest," he continues. "I was very disappointed. And yes, probably a little angry the first night. But that's because I built this up to be more than it should've been. Would I have loved to have the championship? Absolutely. And did I go into the season thinking that it was a must have for my grandfather? Yes."

"That's okay," I insert. "It's understandable. And you've got to know that I hated letting Stan down."

"I know. But I don't want you to feel that way," Nathan says. "You gave us your all, Crew. My grandfather loved watching you play." He stops and clears his throat as if it suddenly got tight. I know mine did.

"He enjoyed this season so much," Nathan says. "Your contribution to all of it was never in question. Not even when the final buzzer went off. I never for a second thought that you let up or that you stopped caring. You're still Crew Fucking McNeill. Bringing you here was probably the best decision I ever made for this team. And I just wanted to say that. And I'm sorry that I haven't said it before this. Michael and Dani kept telling me that you needed some time to process. That you just needed to kind of get over it on your own first. And maybe that's true. But I feel like I should've said this before now."

I'm staring at him, trying to figure out if I am imagining this or if my boss, a man I respect very much, and one of my best friends, has just said some of the best things anyone could've said.

"So you're not saying this because Dani and Michael told you to?"

"No. They thought I should give you more time. They thought I should let you initiate the conversation."

"Wow. Not only are you saying nice things, but you're not listening to Michael."

Nathan nods. "Probably mistakes all around."

I have to grin at that. "Well, here's another big surprise for us both—Michael was wrong."

Nathan actually cracks a smile at that. "Yeah?"

"Yeah. I'm glad you wanted to talk. I love playing for your team, Mr. Armstrong. And I love making this life with you, Nathan. Thank you for this."

For just a second, he looks taken aback. And I realize that the Nathan Armstrong that I met when I first signed with the Racketeers is not the same man I'm looking at now. This man is much softer. More open. Happier.

And I know the woman who is responsible for that. For *us*.

I love her with everything I've got.

But I'd like to think that maybe I'm just a little bit of it too.

"I need to get going or I'm going to be late," Nathan finally says. "Take care of our girl tonight."

"Absolutely," I promise. "See you when you get home."

Nathan heads for the car at the curb where Andrew waits to take him to wherever this meeting is.

I turn and head back inside. Dani and I have the house to ourselves now. But she's upstairs writing and I don't want to interrupt. This new publishing deal of hers is amazing. We're all so proud of her and we know that once the baby comes, her schedule is going to change a lot, so she's trying to get as much writing done as she can now.

I settle back down on the couch and flip through the channels, finding an old sports movie I love about halfway in.

But it's only ten minutes before I hear soft footsteps coming down the stairs.

I pause the movie and look over as she pads across the room to me. She's dressed in silky, loose lounge pants and a matching silky top. I can tell she doesn't have a bra on because her breasts are pressing against the front of the flimsy material. She looks relaxed and a little tired, but she gives me a soft smile.

"Hey, pretty girl," I greet.

"Hey." She sinks down onto the couch and immediately pivots so that she's lying back with her head in my lap.

I drop a hand to her head and start stroking my fingers through her hair. "How was the writing?"

Her eyes slide shut, and she gives a contented sigh as my fingers slide over her scalp. "Great. I finished the chapter. But I'm definitely done for the day."

"Yeah?"

"Yep."

"Okay, then." I reach for my phone. "Do you want cheeseburgers or nachos?"

Her eyes open wide and she looks up at me. "You mean it?"

"Of course."

"Michael's been really adamant about vegetables and stuff."

I grin at her and pull my fingers through her hair. "I'm not Michael." I lean over and brush my lips against hers. "And neither of your overprotective, bossy husbands are here, are they?"

"No, they're not," she whispers against my lips.

"It's just me. Your super fun, extra naughty, always up for a good time boyfriend. And I'm going to spoil you and feed you junk food, and massage your entire body, and we're just going to lie here on this couch and watch stupid TV."

"Oh. My. God," she says softly. "I'm so madly in love with you."

I chuckle and kiss her again.

"I've missed you," she says, running a hand over my stubbled jaw. "I feel like we haven't had enough time, just us."

That makes my heart squeeze.

Our foursome works very well. In fact, I would say all four of us agree that it needs to be all four of us to work at all long term.

However, living with three other adults is a lot sometimes and we all know that we need time on our own here and there.

We also know that we each need time one on one with Danielle. She's the love of my life. I really like Nathan and

Michael and I especially like what they do for her, but I will never give up a chance to be with her by myself.

"I'm looking forward to having you to myself," I tell her.

"I'm glad." She pauses. "And my answer is both."

"Both what?"

"Cheeseburgers *and* nachos."

I grin down at her and run my hand down to rest on her belly.

"Michael's also very concerned about my calorie intake. I figure that won't be a problem if we get both."

"I can definitely get you calories," I tell her.

"And fun." She sighs. "I *love* Nathan and Michael so much, but they've been so intense. I know you and I can just relax tonight, and I'm *so* ready for that."

"You don't want to talk about baby stuff?"

She shakes her head. "No. Is that okay? I feel like that's all we talk about around here."

"Sure, that's totally okay. I want you to know that I'm always happy to talk about it, but if you need a break from it, I'm good for that, too."

"Thank you. I definitely want to talk to you about it sometimes. Just…not tonight."

I stroke my hand back and forth across her stomach. The baby bump is evident now, and I love the way I can cup her belly with my hand.

She rests her hand on mine. "Do you want to talk about hockey? Or the last game?"

I blow out a breath. "I really don't. Is that okay?"

"Totally okay. You know I'm here if you want to talk."

"I actually want to focus on the things that are more important than hockey," I tell her, moving my hand over her belly. "The weddings, the baby, everything has made me realize that yes, I love hockey and I want to keep playing and I really feel like I have some of my best seasons ahead, but…it's not everything anymore, Dani. I've got so much more than that to think about and love."

She squeezes my hand. "I'm so glad you feel that way." She

pauses, then adds, "But I love watching you play and you are so hot when you're on the ice, so you need to keep playing."

I lean over and kiss her deeply. "Yeah, okay, just for you, sweet girl. Though I'm pretty hot off the ice as well."

She giggles and kisses me back and in that moment it hits me that this baby could be mine and I can't take a deep breath for a second.

It's not the first time it's occurred to me, of course, and none of us actually care whose baby it is. We are all equally committed to this family, no matter whose actual DNA ended up mixing with Dani's. But for some reason, in this moment, it grips me especially hard.

This growing belly on this gorgeous, sweet, loving, amazing woman could be *my* baby.

And Dani puts up with all of my crap. My pouting after this loss, the fact that I wasn't ready to get married when everyone else was, the fact that I freaked out about the pregnancy at first.

She loved me through all of it. She accepted me wherever I was at, she was fine with whatever I was ready for, as long as we were together.

And it's in that moment, talking about nachos and just chilling on our couch, that I realize I will never be happy without her. I will never not want to be with her. There will never be a time when this—all of this, the home with Michael and Nathan, the baby, ordering nachos instead of salads—will not be exactly what I want.

I need to marry this girl.

Soon.

I lift my head and run my hand over her cheek. "Okay, I'm ordering the food."

"But it's our secret," she says, batting her eyelashes at me. "You can't tell Michael."

She knows very well that she has me wrapped tightly around her little finger and there's no way that I'm ever going to tell on her.

"Of course. I will get rid of all of the takeout containers before they get home. And if anything gets spilled, or they have any inkling that any contraband came into this house, I'll take the fall."

She snuggles in closer, pressing her cheek against my abs. "You're my favorite co-conspirator."

I chuckle as I type our order into my phone. "You're my favorite everything," I tell her.

"Am I your favorite person to eat eggrolls with?"

I laugh. "You need eggrolls too? Because yes, the answer is yes."

"Let's say the baby needs eggrolls," she says with a little giggle.

I open the app again and add eggrolls.

Once the order is placed, I toss my phone aside and pick up the remote. "So what are you in the mood for?" I ask, pointing it at the TV and pulling up all the streaming apps.

"Hmmm." She pushes up to sit, then stretches, the silky material of the shirt moving over her breasts and baring a strip of stomach. "Well, I've been sitting for awhile, so I was thinking I should do a little stretching." She gives me a look. "Maybe some yoga."

I narrow my eyes. "Yoga? Are you supposed to do that?"

"Definitely. It's *very* good for me. In fact, the more flexible my hips and pelvis are through the pregnancy, the easier delivery will be. I've read all about it."

I say, "Is that right?"

I know exactly what she's doing. Dani and I have done yoga together before. It's good for me too. But we never make it all the way through a session with all of our clothes on. Not once.

She gets up and moves in front of the couch, getting down onto the floor, sitting cross-legged, facing me.

"Dani," I say softly, but firmly.

She meets my gaze. "Yes?"

"We don't have to have sex." I mean it. I always love having her to myself, but we can be close in so many ways. I love just having *time* with her. When we go to the movies, when we go to basketball games, when we have late night snacks in the kitchen and just talk after the other two are asleep.

"I know." She gives me a grin. "But I want to."

This girl was made for a poly relationship, I swear. I don't remember the last time Dani wasn't in the mood for sex and all three of us guys have commented at various times that we truly don't know how one man could keep up with Dani. She's a fucking dream come true.

I grin back. "What if I want to just cuddle?"

She can also always talk me into *anything*, and talking me into sex takes about two seconds. I just want to be sure she knows that I don't need that to want to be with her.

"That's fine." She lifts a shoulder. "I'll just do a little yoga until the food gets here and we can cuddle after we eat."

Uh, huh. "Sounds good." I settle back on the couch, stretching my arms along the back cushions.

She pulls her legs up so the soles of her feet are together and then bends forward. "The yoga is really good to keep my pelvic floor flexible. The articles I've read say that will make delivery easier."

I shake my head. I know what she's doing. But I'll play with her. The three of us all make love to Dani differently. Nathan is the bossy, dominant one. Dani definitely gets off on that. Michael is the intense romantic. She loves that. And I'm the playful flirt. She absolutely loves the way we tease.

"Your pelvic floor, huh?"

"Yep. My vaginal muscles. Obviously, they need to be as flexible as possible to make things easier."

I feel *my* pelvic muscles tighten. "I'm aware of what your pelvic floor is, Dani," I tell her. "It's one of my favorite parts of you."

Her head is bent over her ankles, but I hear her giggle.

"And I guess getting knocked up by one of two pretty big guys means that baby might be good sized," I muse. "Probably makes sense to be sure you're able to really open up."

She looks up. "Exactly my thoughts."

"But," I tell her. "I also know that you're getting good and stretched out on a regular basis."

She gives me a grin as she sits up and then bends her torso to one side, her shirt riding up. "But it's important to stretch *every night*. And my *husbands* won't be home until late. So, I don't know what I'm going to do about that."

I shift as my cock lets me know he knows *exactly* what to do about it. "Our food will be here in about 20 minutes," I remind her.

She grins. "It doesn't have to be a long stretching session."

There is never a time I don't like playing and having sex with Dani, but the times she initiates it are some of the best.

"You have some other appetites that need to be taken care of besides a craving for nachos, pretty girl?" My voice has dropped to a rough timbre.

She bites her bottom lip and nods. "I do."

"You have *two* husbands, and even that isn't enough for you?"

I see the way her eyes spark at this new fun game we've started to play at times.

I don't feel nearly as weird about being the boyfriend as I expected. I haven't been left out of anything, and everything at home has seemed just like usual.

"I'm just very needy," she says, bending the other way now. "I think I'm wearing them out. They're both a little older than me and they both have very important jobs, so they're not here all the time, so what am I supposed to do when they're not here to take care of me?" She links her fingers together and stretches them overhead, arching her back.

I focus on her gorgeous tits and the hardened nipples pressing against the front of her silky shirt. Though I do wish Nathan was here to hear her say that he's too old to keep up with her.

"Well, I suppose I could send you upstairs to one of those big, thick, vibrating dildos you've got."

"I could do that, and just think about what it would be like to have you filling me up instead…"

"You could. That's probably what you should do. Even though you should be fantasizing about your husbands. I guess that way at least you're not spreading your legs for another man."

"Hmm," she hums, straightening and running her tongue over her bottom lip. "But that makes *them* so hot and possessive." She brings a hand up to cup one breast. "I love when they watch me get fucked by someone else."

I pull in a long breath. We've been sharing her for months now. We *live* together. She's pregnant, for God's sake. And still, all of this is so hot. "Did you come down here to seduce me, Mrs. Armstrong?"

Her name isn't legally Armstrong. Because it was a commitment ceremony rather than a legal marriage, technically, her last name is still Larkin. But she wants to change her name. She actually wants it to be Armstrong Hughes McNeill but that seems like a lot.

Though I know Nathan and Michael love the idea of her with their last name as much as I do. And, of course, we'd have to have some combination of the three.

Probably.

Fuck, this is just one of the things about a poly relationship that takes more work than a traditional one-on-one pairing.

Still, right now, calling her *Mrs.* makes our playtime hotter.

"I did," she admits. "I'm hungry, but not just for food." She squeezes her breast and slides her other hand over her stomach to her pussy, running her finger over the silk covering her center. "Please help me out."

"Naughty girl, you don't even have panties on right now, do you?"

"No." She smiles sweetly. "I'm just hanging out at home, having a quiet night in."

"Oh, you intend to be quiet?"

"Of course. Why would I be loud?"

"Because if I'm going to fuck another man's wife, I'm gonna want to hear her screaming my name." She sucks in a little breath as I sit forward, resting my forearms on my thighs. "Will you scream my name for me, Mrs. Armstrong?"

"Let's find out," she says with a sassy smile.

With that, I'm up off the couch and stalking toward her.

"Take your clothes off," I tell her, towering over her. I strip my shirt off, tossing it on the couch.

She quickly does the same with her shirt, then gets on her knees, sliding her pants off and revealing she really isn't wearing panties.

"Hands and knees," I tell her, kneeling. "Let's get you good and stretched out."

"Yes, please."

I run a hand over her sweet ass and give it a smack. She moans. I slide my hand between her legs and cup her wet, hot, bare pussy. I circle her clit, and then slide two fingers deep.

"Jesus, you're soaking."

She presses up against my hand. "I want you so much. I want to be fucked well, fed well, and then just sack out on this couch to fall asleep to a movie before being carried up to bed like a princess."

I love that she knows what she wants and knows she can tell me all of it. And I can take care of all of those things. "Giving you exactly what you want and need is the pleasure of my life, sweet girl," I tell her as I pump my fingers into her pussy.

She cups one breast, tugging on the nipple and moaning. "Everything is so much more sensitive. I feel like I can't get enough."

"God, you're gorgeous and fucking needy as hell. You're going to be a great quick little fuck here, aren't you?"

She gives a moan and says *yes*, breathlessly.

I drag her wetness over her clit, circling, hard and fast as she pants.

I run a hand up her back, then around to play with her other nipple. She immediately arches closer to my touch.

"Crew, God, that feels good," she tells me, her voice husky.

"God, I wanna keep playing with you, but we don't have much time," I tell her as the need to sink deep suddenly grips me hard.

"I need it hard and fast," she tells me.

I shake my head with a smile. Our shy girl has definitely blossomed into a sex goddess. She's submissive to everything we ever want to do and try, but she's greedy and can be demanding at times, too.

"Crew," she pleads, wiggling her ass. "Please."

"So greedy," I tease. "I want to lay back and pull you down on my face. I want to slide my cock into this demanding little mouth and put it to work. I want to spank you and fuck you with a dildo to remind you who's really in charge here."

"No!" she protests, starting to turn. "I want—"

But I move to grip the back of her neck, keeping her on her hands and knees and quieting her.

"I know exactly what you want and you're lucky that I'm the easy-going one who would walk over hot coals for you because I'm going to give you exactly what you're asking for," I tell her, lowering my shorts, and lining my cock up with her pussy. "I'm so wrapped up in you, I have no hope of ever denying you a thing." Then I thrust and sink deep.

She moans and presses back against me.

I reach around and find her clit, realizing that I'm not going to be able to take long, sweet strokes. I need to give her exactly what she wants. Every time. Nathan and Michael can boss her and even chastise her and give her rules. Me? I'm putty in her hands. No matter what.

I thrust hard. "Is this what you want, greedy girl?"

"Yes, oh my God, Crew."

I keep moving, getting lost in her body as I always do.

Sex has never been like this with anyone else, and I will never, ever crave another woman in my life. Danielle is everything I will ever need.

I pump faster and harder.

"I'm so close, I'm so close," she pants.

I pull out suddenly, needing to shift her so I can go hard and deep. She's bracing herself with her hands, and I need more leverage.

I move her to the couch, laying her upper body over the cushions, then grip her hips and thrust deep again.

"*Crew.*"

I run my hand from her hip, over the swell of her belly, feeling emotion tighten my chest, then to her clit. The changes in her body make me feel possessive and protective.

"Fuck yes," I grit through my teeth as I feel her pussy tighten around me. "Come for me Dani."

I circle harder, thrust deeper, and then she's coming, her pussy clenching and milking me. "Crew!"

I let go in the next moment, filling her up, heat and pleasure streaking through me.

"Fuck. Yes Dani. I love you so damn much."

She's breathing hard, pressing back against me as the ripples continue through her body and she comes down from her orgasm.

I just hold her like that for a long moment before I finally pull out and then climb up onto the couch, pulling her with me. I kiss her hair, then her neck, then her shoulder, holding her against me.

I love feeling her breathing fast, her heartbeat thundering against my hand, her warm, sweet body curling into mine.

"Oh, yes. That was exactly what I needed." She breathes out happily.

I chuckle and nuzzle my face into her hair. "Glad I could help."

"You are always exactly what I need," she says, squeezing my arms.

"Good. But now we should get dressed before the food gets

here. Or you need to at least get under a blanket. I don't want anyone sneaking a peek."

She laughs.

"What?"

"It's just funny when you and Nathan and Michael say things like that, considering, you know, you all share me with two other guys."

I reach down and pinch her ass. "Two other *specific* guys. That doesn't mean just *anyone* can look."

She turns her head and kisses my cheek. "I love you."

"I love you too."

I stand, scoop her up, and head for the powder room off the kitchen. We clean up before pulling our clothes back on before settling back on the couch, her tucked up under my arm, her head resting on my chest.

I want to propose to her.

Right now.

But something holds me back.

I want it to be special. A huge grand gesture. Completely over the top.

That is what she deserves. Especially after I made her wait. Especially after I seemed so unsure. I need to make sure she understands that I mean every single word and that when I say forever, I absolutely mean fucking *forever*.

That means I need to come up with something that shows that I put a ton of thought into it, and that it was a definite plan and not a spontaneous moment after sex.

And I need to talk to the guys.

Not to get their permission, because I know that they want this to happen. But because I want them to help me plan something.

That's how we do things now. We're Cookie and Company.

And even if I was slow to get my shit together, I am definitely a part of this company.

"I love you so damn much," I tell her, kissing the top of her head. "You know that, right?"

"Of course I do." She tips her head to look up at me. "I love you so much, too."

And I realize looking at her that she's happy. Completely content. Right now, in this moment, with me.

I am able to give her things that the other guys can't. I can be there to chill with her, to play with her, to treat her when the other guys are being intense and responsible and overly protective.

I do have a place here and I not only want to be Dani's third husband, but I think she needs me to be.

"You know what we need?" I ask her.

"A chocolate chip skillet cookie?" she asks.

I laugh, not because how much this girl is eating suddenly is funny, but because that was *exactly* what I was thinking. "Yes," I tell her. "With vanilla ice cream and hot fudge."

She nods. "You are the perfect man."

I laugh and reach for my phone to place the dessert order.

"But remember, you can't tell Michael," she says, tucking her feet up underneath her butt.

I look over at her. "If you think that Michael doesn't know that you and I are going to eat junk food tonight, you don't know him very well."

She laughs, but looks happier than I have ever seen her. "You've got a point. It'll be worth the extra salad he'll make me eat in the next couple of days, though."

"He'll *encourage* you to eat," I say. Michael would never dictate her diet.

"Yes. Encourage," she agrees.

"And you do it because it makes *him* feel better because he's taking care of you."

She nods. "I think he and Nathan are both feeling a little anxious right now because they're so happy about the baby and they want everything to go well and they want *me* to be happy and feel good, but there's only so much they can do. Right now, for the next few months, it's really just me and my body taking care of this kid."

I lift her hand to my lips and kiss her knuckles. "You're right. That makes all of us feel a little unsure. We want to be a part of it, but there's only so much we can do."

"I know. I get that. And it's sweet. But either one of them as a husband and soon-to-be-father would be a lot." She sighs. "And I have them both." Her expression holds love *and* exasperation.

I give her a smile. I know exactly what she means. "They're lucky they found you," I said. "Someone who can put up with all of that energy and who can take in all of that love and just give it right back to them."

Her face softens, and she smiles. "Thank you for saying that."

"We're all very lucky to have you, Dani. Thanks for putting up with us. In all the ways we are each a lot."

"I wouldn't have any of you any way other than how you are," she says, and I know she means it. "And *thank you* for being the one that will never, ever make me eat a salad."

I laugh. We eat plenty of salads around here, even when she's not pregnant. During the season, I try to keep my diet pretty clean and healthy. But I'm definitely her enabler. Any cookie, pizza, or french fry this woman wants, I will get her. And I'll fight anyone who tries to stand in my way.

I will happily keep that role for the rest of our lives.

Because this is what we *all* need—the balance, each of us in different roles, all of us separate pieces that fit together to make a bigger picture.

Like just as I know Michael will make me eat salad for the next couple of days, too, I also ordered two extra skillet cookies for the guys.

CHAPTER 9
Michael

"YOU NEED to chop those tomatoes smaller," my mother says as she eyes my cutting board.

"Yes, ma'am," I say automatically, going back over the tomatoes for a second pass with the knife. I'm making three different salsas using fresh ingredients from our garden for a Fourth of July gathering. We have a slew of family and friends coming over in about an hour, and I have a whole charcuterie spread underway.

Later on, I'll be firing up the grill and making burgers and barbecue chicken and I'm one hundred percent in my element. There's a pitcher of lemonade on the island and cupcakes from Luna decorated with red and blue stars. I love everything about entertaining and sharing a day with my favorite people.

My mother gives a murmur of approval and returns to the breakfast nook table, where Dani, Luna, and Lori McNeill are all cooing and fussing over our next-door neighbor Marissa's new baby.

My wife is holding the baby tenderly, smiling and making faces at him, even though he's asleep. Dani runs a finger down his cheek and I see her wedding bands resting on her delicate ring finger.

Wife.

God, I love the sound of that.

Dani is past the morning sickness and she looks radiant in a blue sundress, her hair piled up on her head in a messy bun in protest against the heat. The sundress hides her bump, but there's no hiding her fuller breasts and luminous skin. She looks perfect holding a baby and some days I have to damn near pinch myself over the reality that in a few months she'll be holding *our* baby.

Marissa's husband Mark is helping me with the salsas. We've been sharing gardening duties all summer. Mark loves to water the plants and I'm happy to let him. I think it gives him a moment of respite from his growing family, which includes a three-year-old daughter Gracie and a pug, along with their newborn son, Romeo. I love that Romeo and our baby will grow up as playmates and that we're establishing friendships with the neighbors.

"What do you think?" Mark asks me. "Is this enough cilantro?" He has a massive pile chopped and ready to go.

"You can never have too much cilantro. Unless you're Crew. He hates it. We should leave it out of the pico de gallo so he can eat it."

"I'll give the guy whatever he wants, or doesn't want, since he's entertaining my daughter and my dog," Mark says, gesturing with his knife to our backyard. "He's a human jungle gym out there."

The windows are open and I can see and hear Crew and Gracie. Crew is taking turns throwing a ball to the dog and tossing Gracie up into the air.

The second he sets Gracie down, her little toddler voice shrieks, "Do it again!"

"Okay, I'll do it again." Crew is laughing and smiling and doesn't even sound out of breath. He throws her so high I'm momentarily worried she'll get scared but she seems delighted and he catches her easily. Then he bounces her up and down before pretending to eat her ear. She laughs hysterically. The dog barks. It's a perfect summer scene.

"He's definitely a kid at heart," I tell Mark. He's going to be the fun dad. There's absolutely no doubt about that. Piggybacks, tickling, and sports. Nathan will be the one spoiling our baby, I'll be the voice of reason, the bath and storytime dad. Dani will offer unconditional love and all the hugs and kisses a child could ever want.

We all bring something different to the table and I love that. We're all going to love this baby with our whole hearts though and I can't wait to meet the little guy or girl. I've had a moment or two of anxiety that something would go wrong with the pregnancy but now that Dani is in her second trimester and everyone knows our good news, I'm just looking forward to the future, while enjoying the now.

"My back hurts just watching him." Mark dumps the cilantro into two of the mixing bowls. "He's saving me a fortune in chiropractic bills. I'm forty and I'm parenting on caffeine and a hope and a prayer. It was all fun and games having a hot younger wife until she wanted to have kids. Now I'm just a broken man."

That makes me laugh.

Marissa calls out in a teasing voice, "Excuses, Mark. No one wants to hear them. I carried and gave birth to your children, remember?"

"If I could have given birth for you, honey, I would have," he says calmly. He turns to me and mouths, "*No, I wouldn't,*" while shaking his head.

Marissa rolls her eyes.

"Crew has always had a lot of energy," Lori says. "I picture him wrestling with kids, which I absolutely cannot picture Nathan doing. Speaking of, where is Nathan?"

"He's upstairs draining the hot tub," I tell her.

"Now?" Dani asks, looking as bewildered as I felt when he told me his plan twenty minutes ago.

I just shrug. "He's worried about safety." Nathan has been on full-blown safety patrol this past week, as if we don't have months still to get ready. I'm not about to interfere. He's a control freak and he needs to do something to feel a part of this pregnancy, so this is his way of contributing.

"Dani, you have to learn something about men," Lori says. "During any party prep, a woman will be running around like a chicken with its head cut off, doing things that actually matter, and a man will choose that very moment to conquer the least important thing on his honey-do list from the entire last year."

"Exactly," my mother agrees with a firm nod. "I'd be scrubbing bathrooms and Clayton would decide that is when he needs to go through old boxes in the attic or leaf blow the woods behind the house. The woods, for goodness' sake. Where leaves actually belong."

That is true, my father did do that right before my sister Teresa's graduation party, but I also feel the need to defend at least myself and my neighbor, if not the whole of my gender.

"Maybe that's a generation thing because Mark and I are in the kitchen while you ladies are all sitting there sipping lemonade," I point out.

"Yeah," Mark says. "Exactly. And Crew is watching the kid."

"Nathan is the same age as Mark," Dani says. "I don't think you can call it a generational thing."

I grin at her. "Nor does Nathan ever do anything he can pay someone to do." This is purely him working out his sense of helplessness over the pregnancy and impatience for the baby's arrival.

Mark is now chopping onions and his eyes are red and tearing up.

"Babe, are you crying?" Marissa asks, standing up and coming over to him, trying to hold back a grin. "That's so cute."

"Yes, because I'm devastated by how little you appreciate me."

Mark's sense of humor always amuses me. Marissa is giving him a kiss on the cheek now and grabbing a grape to pop into her husband's mouth. I'm about to comment when the back door opens. Crew has Gracie in his arms.

"Nate is flooding the backyard," he says. "Like, legitimately flooding it. Take monkey girl here so I can run upstairs and let him know this is not the time to do whatever idiotic thing he's doing."

"Here, I'll take her," Luna says, holding her arms out for Gracie.

Gracie leaps into the air with no fear that she won't be caught. Fortunately, Luna manages to wrangle her into her arms before setting her down on the floor. The three-year-old runs over to her parents. "Cheese!" she demands.

Lori laughs. "A girl after my own heart."

I set my knife down and decide to follow Crew upstairs. I don't think Crew knows Nathan is draining the hot tub and I have a feeling he isn't going to be thrilled about it.

"Where the hell is the couch?" Crew asks as we go through the living room to the stairs.

I eye the gaping hole in our front room. "He said it's a suffocation hazard for the baby. It got hauled away an hour ago. I guess he has new sofas on order."

"That's some bullshit right there," Crew says. "He's not the only one who lives here. And seriously, that needed to happen today?"

He's not wrong.

Crew loved that couch. It was his choice to have a giant sofa that allowed all four of us to lounge on it at the same time. I get where Nathan is coming from—the sections of the sofa could slide apart and a child could get wedged down between them, but he's going a little overboard at this point.

Crew pauses to eye the baby gate that was also just installed. "How does this open?"

"There's a latch."

He tries to open it but fails. He decides to just vault over it and takes the steps two at a time.

I reach out and click it open before ascending the first step behind him.

Dani is now behind me, Romeo sleeping her arms, but I pause

and lean down to give her a kiss. "Go relax, sweetheart. We'll be back in a minute."

"I don't want them to butt heads," she says, biting her bottom lip.

That makes me grin. "Too late for that. They thrive on butting heads. It's their entertainment. Seriously, stay with our guests."

Dani nods. "Okay." She gives me a smile. "Isn't Romeo beautiful?"

"Not as beautiful as you, Cookie."

She laughs. "Thank you, Michael." She rocks Romeo in her arms. "Can you believe we're having one of these?"

I cup her cheeks and kiss her on the forehead. "I'm grateful for it every minute of every day since we found out."

She sways one more time before giving me a smile and heading back to the kitchen.

Damn. My heart is so full.

The feeling evaporates when I go out on our upper deck and see Crew waving his arms around angrily at Nathan.

"Tell him, Doc," Crew says, turning to me for back up. "He can't just drain *my* hot tub an hour before a party without talking to me about it."

"I don't have to talk to you about draining *our* hot tub. It's a safety hazard."

I'm not sure which issue to address first, so I start with the obvious and easier one. I glance over the side of the deck, seeing that a hose has been connected and is in fact dumping a river of chemically laden water onto the grass I just managed to coax into green lushness. I pull it out of the hot tub to stop the flooding. "Nathan, it's flooding the yard. We're having people over. It's ruining the grass, and it's filled with chemicals. There are supposed to be kids playing in that grass later."

For a second, Nathan looks poised to argue. But then he glances over the railing and down into the yard. "I thought it would disperse more than it did," he admits gruffly.

"You can't just go sticking hoses in shit and throwing out

couches in our house without discussing it with us, *Boss*." Crew's emphasis on the last word is sarcastic and angry.

"Safety doesn't require a committee."

"The baby isn't coming for another six months and won't be moving around on her own for another six months. That's an entire year where I can still enjoy my hot tub," Crew says. His voice and expression are frustrated. "Do you even know anything about babies?"

It strikes a nerve with Nathan. He crosses his arms over his navy golf shirt and narrows his eyes. "What do *you* know about babies?"

"I have a huge family with lots of cousins. Unlike you, I've been around babies."

"Thank you for pointing out that I have no family. I don't exactly need a reminder, McNeill. But I've been doing research."

Shit. I'm about to intervene when Crew sighs and shakes his head.

"Nate, I'm sorry, I didn't mean it like that. I'm not trying to rub your face in anything. I'm just saying that you can't act like you're the only father here. We're *all* this baby's father and we need to talk about stuff."

"Are you going to be a father?" Nathan asks him.

There's no censure. He just sounds curious.

"It's a fair question," I say. "We're not exactly sure where you stand, Crew."

"Just because I didn't want to get married doesn't mean I'm bailing on my responsibilities as a father. I'm here. I want this. I want to be a part of all of this." He sweeps his arms wide to gesture at the house and the yard. "I want this baby and I want to be a father. But for fuck's sake, I need you to treat me like a man. Not a kid. I am *not* a kid. I'm not going to be the fun uncle to our baby. I'm a father, too. And so is Doc, Nathan."

Nathan doesn't say anything for a heartbeat. Then he nods. "You're right. I'm not the only father."

Crew's mouth splits into a grin. "What did you say?" He cups his hand to his ear. "I need to hear that again."

"I said I'm not the only father. You are both the father of this baby as well and I shouldn't be making changes to the house without talking to you both and Danielle."

"That's not the part I need repeated. I want you to hear that first part again."

"You're right. There. Are you happy? Part of my soul just died, but I admit it, you were right, I was wrong."

"God, I wish I had recorded that on my phone," Crew says.

I eye the half-filled hot tub and look down at my soggy yard. "Are we all good then? Everyone agrees this was unfortunate timing and we should get back to hosting a kick-ass cookout for our friends and family?"

Crew nods. "Hell, yeah."

Nathan nods too. "Yes." He claps Crew on the shoulder. "I'm glad you're all in."

"Thank you." Crew gets serious again. "I am one hundred percent all in. I want this baby. I want Dani. I want us. If you ever doubt any of that at any point, please come talk to me first before making assumptions."

"We will do that," I assure him. "We all need to check in with each other if we ever have any concerns. That's what we do. We talk. We're a family."

"Understood." Nathan rubs his jaw.

"You owe me five grand for that couch," Crew says. "I fucking loved that couch."

"You owe me new grass," I tell Nathan. "That was brand new sod and half of it is currently floating away down the side of the house."

"Is this a bad time to mention that I may or may not have been looking at bigger houses with less stairs?" Nathan asks, breaking out into a grin.

"Oh, hell, no," I tell him. "We are not moving. I love this street and all our neighbors."

One of our other neighbors, Peter, who is a retired British real estate developer, chooses that moment to yell up, "Ahoy, neighbors! Your yard looks like I could take a skiff out onto it and drop a line for trout."

I laugh, in spite of my irritation about my lawn. "See?" I tell Nathan. "This is fun, right, having neighbors?"

"It's a fucking blast." But he's fighting a smile.

Crew leans over the railing and shouts down, "Getting a little wet never hurt anyone, Peter."

"That's what she said!" Peter calls back up.

Crew almost chokes on his laughter.

"Oh, dear God," Nathan mutters, shaking his head. "Bev must be a patient woman."

"Bev is a cougar," Crew says. "Have you seen the way she looks at Michael?"

He's right. Peter's wife has a way of looking at me that makes me feel like I forgot to put a shirt on. "She's harmless. I think."

We all exit the deck and start to file down the hallway.

"You said 'she,'" Nathan says to Crew. "Do you think it's a girl?"

Crew shrugs. "Did I? I don't know. I haven't thought about it, but now that you say that, maybe I do kind of feel like it's a girl. It doesn't matter either way to me, though."

"What do you think?" Nathan asks me.

I consider it. "I don't get a feeling one way or the other. I just want a healthy baby."

Nathan nods. "Me, too."

The doorbell is ringing when we're heading back downstairs. I hear my mother call out that she'll get it.

When we reach the bottom of the stairs, Nathan tries to open the baby gate. "Do I squeeze or do I lift? I can't remember."

"I have no idea," Crew says. "Move so I can just step over it."

"No, I almost have it." Nathan shakes and rattles it.

"I think you just squeeze it," I say, reaching around him so I can try it. Nathan's hand is in the way. "Do something, this is awkward."

"This house has so many stairs," Lori laments, hands on her hips, watching us as we're all fighting over the latch on the baby gate. "You're going to need half a dozen of these gates."

"See?" Nathan says in triumph, rattling the gate again aggressively before finally giving up and climbing over the gate. "I told you this house has too many fucking stairs! At least Lori agrees with me."

"Fucking stairs," Gracie yells, skidding past us in her sundress, a slice of cheese in her hand.

Marissa glares at Nathan.

"Oh, sh—I mean, sorry." He makes a face. "Didn't know she was here."

I undo the latch and exit the stairwell, struck again by how large and empty our living room looks without Crew's monstrosity of a couch.

"You're going to have to clean up your act before the baby is born," my mother says, walking past us to answer the door. "All of you."

"Fucking damn it!" Mark yells from the kitchen. He's waving his hand when we all turn our heads on a swivel. "Cut my finger. I'm fine, though." He pops his finger in his mouth.

Dani emerges from the powder room. "What did I miss?"

The front door opens and Owen Phillips comes in with his son and a teenage girl. I see Crew's father, who drove separately to pick up a few things, behind them. William seems to have his arms filled with yard toys.

"Nothing, Cookie. Just happy chaos."

Crew made it clear he's here for the long haul and I'm relieved and thrilled. Our girl needs to know that, too, and it's what she wants.

All of us.

It's what I want too.

CHAPTER 10

Crew

"DANIELLE LARKIN," Dani says to the receptionist as we approach the desk.

Nathan makes a sound in the back of his throat.

I glance over at him. He looks irritated and I'm not exactly sure why.

"I just need you to fill out these forms and I'll need to see your insurance card," the receptionist says with a smile. She looks around mine and Dani's age.

We're at the medical center for Dani's first ultrasound appointment. Michael is coming straight from work and meeting us here, though he hasn't arrived yet. Nathan spent the morning at home with us.

"I don't have insurance," Dani says, taking the clipboard from the receptionist.

Honestly, that's news to me. We've never discussed it and I've always had insurance, so I realize I take it for granted.

"Oh, well, um, I don't think that was clear when the appointment was made," the receptionist says. "You're going to have to talk to our financial consultant before you do the ultrasound."

"Why?" Nathan demands. "I'll just pay out-of-pocket for it."

The girl looks taken aback. "Well... that has to be paid for then before the appointment and you still need to speak to the consultant because there are different pay scales based on financial need so we'll have to reschedule..." Her voice trails off and her eyes widen when Nathan pulls out his wallet and opens it to reveal a fat wad of cash.

"We're not rescheduling the appointment," he tells her firmly.

Now the poor girl just looks scared.

"Just give us a second," I tell her, giving her a reassuring smile. "Dani, why don't you have a seat, sweetheart, and fill out the medical history forms."

She nods and goes to sit down, clipboard in hand.

Nathan looks poised to go another round with the receptionist but I gesture for him to step to the side. "Relax," I tell him. "You're freaking that poor girl out. You look like a drug dealer or a mafia boss waving hundred-dollar bills at her."

He snaps his wallet shut. "Shit, I do, don't I?"

"Yes. Just let me handle this right now. Then we need to figure out how to add Dani to your insurance as a domestic partner or whatever before the next appointment."

Dani isn't legally married to either Nathan or Michael because she didn't want to have to choose between them, but there are clearly practical issues arising from that. I'm surprised Michael didn't address the issue before but hell, maybe the three of them have discussed all of this and didn't include me in that conversation since I'm not her husband. I don't know. But right now, we need to get this ultrasound handled as planned without Nathan bullying a girl just trying to do her job.

"Hi," I say to the girl as I approach the desk again, giving her a big smile. "Sorry about that. We didn't realize there was a protocol we had to follow. We would prefer not to reschedule so can I just pay out-of-pocket with no financial assistance?" I pull out my debit card and hand it to her. "It doesn't matter what it is. Then maybe you can help me set up a meeting with the financial consultant so we can get this sorted before Danielle's next appointment? I would really appreciate it."

She is studying my debit card. "You're Crew McNeill? The Racketeers Crew McNeill?"

"That's me. You a hockey fan?"

"Yes. So much," she gushes.

"Sorry about the championship," I tell her, giving her a sheepish shrug. "We'll bring it home next year."

"Oh, absolutely. I know you will." She clutches my debit card to her chest for a split second before she seems to realize what she's doing. "I'm a fan, no matter what. I'll get this taken care of. Just give me five. I need to ask my manager what code to put in my computer."

"Thank you, that's fantastic. What's your name?"

"Kayla."

"Thank you, Kayla."

She nods, pushes her chair back on its wheels and quickly stands up. "I'll be right back."

When I go over and sit with Dani and Nathan, he's looking stormy.

I give him a knock-it-off look. "This is so exciting, babe," I say, as I sit down on the opposite side of Dani and squeeze her knee. "Our first look at the baby. I can't wait."

She gives me a bright smile. "This is crazy, isn't it? Did you get the bill sorted out?"

I nod. "We need to get you insurance though."

"I'll talk to my lawyer and my assistant," Nathan says. "I should have done that already. I'm sorry, Danielle. I dropped the ball."

Nathan looks like I felt when we lost the championship. Like he's let down all of Chicago.

"Don't worry about it. I didn't even think about it either. I'm never sick so it doesn't really come up and they didn't say anything when we went to the OB/GYN."

Nathan is reading her paperwork on the clipboard. "What's with Larkin? I thought we agreed you're going to be Danielle Armstrong Hughes."

"My name hasn't been legally changed yet. I can't sign in that way."

"Why haven't you changed it? Just because we're not legally married doesn't mean you can't change it."

"I've been writing a book and growing a placenta," she says, cheeks pink.

That color in her face is a sure indication that she's annoyed with Nathan. I have to admit, the guy has terrible timing. This is a happy occasion and he's being territorial. I get it. I'm not exactly fucking thrilled that she's planning on taking Michael and Nathan's last names and not mine, but I have no rational reason to be mad about it. Neither does Nathan. I hate paperwork and standing at the social security office doesn't sound like anything I would want to do when I have a free couple of hours, so I don't blame Dani for not jumping on it. He needs to lay off.

"How about you have your people get everything ready to go so Dani doesn't have to dig around online for all the information on how to do that?" I ask. "Seeing as you love to have your people do shit for you."

Nathan frowns at me. He's about to say something when Kayla the receptionist calls me up to the desk. "Crew, I have your card for you." She gives me a bright smile.

By the time I've signed the receipt and returned to Dani and Nathan, shoving my wallet into the pocket of my shorts, Michael has arrived, thank God. He knows how to rein in the bossy billionaire better than me.

He gives Dani a kiss on her temple and glances at the paperwork. He takes my seat but I don't mind. Doc has a tendency to let me and Nathan take center stage so I work hard to remember to give him his fair share of closeness to our girl.

"Why Armstrong Hughes?" I ask Dani as I slouch in my chair. "Why not Hughes Armstrong?"

"It just sounds better," Michael tells me. "We were going for flow. It doesn't mean anything."

"Hmm." It has me wondering what the baby's last name is

going to be. If Dani's name is theirs, where does my name go? Especially if the baby is mine biologically. I know intellectually it's most likely not since Dani and Michael spent a few days in Vegas together and when they got home, I was on strict orders not to have sex because of a groin strain thanks to that dickhead Justin Travers, who plays for the Dragons. He took a cheap shot and rammed me into the boards for no fucking reason.

Justin Fucking Travers is the reason this baby most likely isn't mine biologically and that makes me wonder again where the hell I fit in. Sure, I can be a father. But not biologically, not legally, not with my name anywhere. I refuse to be a side note to our child.

"Danielle?"

We look up and see a woman in the open doorway, wearing scrubs and glancing around the waiting room.

"That's me." Dani stands up.

We all pop up too and the woman looks a little startled.

"Is everyone coming with you?" she asks, studying our faces like she's trying to figure out who is who and why the hell we're all here.

"Yes, they're all coming in with me."

The tech looks a little annoyed that she's going to have to wrangle a crowd, but she pastes a smile on her face. "Great. I'm Jeanine. Which one of you is Dad?"

"They all are," Dani says, her chin up proudly, and a little defiantly.

There's nothing but silence for a solid five seconds, then Jeanine appears to decide she doesn't care enough to ask for further details because she just repeats, "Great. A couple of you will have to stand."

I open my mouth and Michael gives me a don't-say-anything look, which offends me. I was going to say that was fine, but clearly he was assuming I was going to be an asshole about it. Instead of stating my case for most reasonable boyfriend *ever*, I just very generously take a spot at Dani's feet and let Michael and Nathan file in on the side of her opposite the ultrasound technician. I stick my hands in my pockets because I don't know what to do with them as the tech explains all the machinery and instructs Dani to lift her shirt and roll her leggings down.

It's quiet in the room and when she squirts gel on Dani's stomach, it sounds loud. It also sounds like ketchup or mustard coming out of the bottle and the unwanted thought has me lifting my hand and coughing into it. The enormity of this moment is suddenly making my throat tight.

I pull my phone out and take a few photos of Dani, the guys next to her. I want to capture that look on her face. It's nerves and wonder and excitement as the wand drops onto her belly.

Then we see the image pop up on the screen. There is tapping on the keyboard from the tech and then we hear it.

The heartbeat.

Holy shit...

"There he is," Dani says, head turned toward the screen. "Hi, baby."

Her voice already sounds different. She sounds like a *mother*. I've never been more in love with her than I am right now, seeing her light up at the sound of our baby's heartbeat.

"It sounds strong," Michael says, holding Dani's hand.

Nathan has a hand on her shoulder. He doesn't speak and I can see why. He's fighting with his emotions. His jaw is set and his nostrils are flaring.

I give Dani's foot a squeeze because it's only the part of her accessible to me, but I don't mind because holy shit, that's a baby on the screen.

It looks more like a baby than I was expecting.

"There's the head, obviously, and the spine." There is more clicking and tapping on the keyboard as the tech measures this and that and spouts out things that I'm barely listening to. I hear, "normal, age appropriate, well-developed," and a few other things that make it clear there are no red flags and so I just stare at that screen in total fucking amazement.

It's a baby. Little feet, little fingers, a big head, a tiny button nose. For a brief second, I wonder if the baby looks like me before I recover my sanity. There is no way to tell on this screen. If anything, the baby looks like Stanford, Nathan's grandfather, which isn't even possible since Nathan can't have kids.

"Do we want to know, boy or girl?" Jeanine asks.

The guys and I look to Dani. "It's your decision," I tell her.

Dani quickly shakes her head. "I don't want to know."

"So everything is good?" Nathan asks the tech.

"The doctor will let you know if there is any cause for concern, but everything is measuring the way it should."

Michael is eagle-eyeing the shit out of everything, and he doesn't look alarmed, so I feel reassured that everything is fine.

Jeanine prints out the ultrasound pictures and hands them to Michael. "Here you go. Congratulations, all of you. Danielle, you can get cleaned up and I'll wait for you in the hallway."

She hands a towel to Dani, who mops up her belly. She's doing a half-ass job of it, trying to sit up and see the pictures again. Nathan takes over, wiping her skin with the towel and repeatedly kissing the top of her head.

"Danielle, you're incredible," he tells her. "You're perfect. Everything is perfect. Right, Doc?"

Michael nods. "Everything looks great." But he's staring at the print-out and he's wearing a strange expression.

"What?" I ask in alarm.

"Nothing." He shakes his head. But then he opens his mouth again. "It's just...well, she just handed this to me and I looked at it automatically. I can see the sex of the baby. I looked away when the baby turned on the screen so I wouldn't see, but...now I know."

"Don't tell me," Dani says quickly. "Please, Michael."

"I won't, Cookie."

"Why would that woman do that?" Nathan demands. "Can I see?"

Dani nods. "Yes. Michael shouldn't know without you and

Crew knowing. But don't tell me. Any of you. You have to promise."

"I don't want to know either," I say quickly, because I want to stand in solidarity with Dani. Also, my track record at secret-keeping is spotty.

"I want to know." Nathan takes the length of images from Michael and studies them.

I see understanding dawn on his face. Only I can't tell if it's a boy or girl, just that he knows.

But then he quickly schools his features and grumbles, "Baby Larkin. That's what it says on here. We need to talk about that."

"I agree."

Dani has pulled her leggings back up and smoothed her shirt down. "We do need to talk about that. I think the baby needs to have the same name as the biological father so there aren't any legal issues."

We're all a little surprised because Dani isn't usually so forthright. She tends to defer to us for advice and decisions but things are different now. She's protecting the baby.

It makes me lean down and kiss her, hard. "God, I love you. Yes, you're right. We have to do the smart thing."

"I agree," Michael says. "But I also think that you should legally marry Nathan. You need health insurance and we don't want any legal entanglements if anything ever happens to Nathan."

Nathan looks taken aback, but then he grins. He's pleased with the idea, obviously. "You killing me off, Hughes?"

Michael laughs. "No, of course not. But Dani needs legal protection too. Besides, do you want there to be a legal battle over your assets if anything does happen to you? Relatives will crawl out of the woodwork to claim your money if Dani isn't legally your wife."

Nathan makes a face. "No shit. I want the Racketeers to go to Dani, without question."

"That's sexy, baby," I tell her. "You'll be my boss."

"I should hope to God you're retired by the time I die," Nathan says dryly. "I'm only forty-two for fuck's sake."

"Oh, my God, can we not talk about anyone dying right now, please?" Dani asks, taking Michael's hand and climbing off the table. "Yes, I agree to all of the above. That all makes sense. Now let's go get lunch, please and talk about something fun, like baby names and my baby shower."

That makes me grin.

Mom Dani is more of a ball-buster. I like it. "Yes, ma'am. Whatever you want, Mama."

Michael takes the ultrasound images back from Nathan and tucks them into his pants pocket. "Sounds perfect, Cookie. What do you want for lunch?"

"I want a milkshake and a burger. And cheesy fries."

Oh, she's good. I know exactly what she's doing and these two are totally falling for it.

Michael nods. "Of course. Whatever you want."

"I should ship some of your favorite ice cream up from Franklin," Nathan adds as we all file out of the office.

"Really? That sounds amazing," Dani says, giving his hand a squeeze. "And can you rub my back tonight?"

"Absolutely."

"You're a dirty, naughty girl," I murmur in her ear. "I love it."

She shoots me a secret sexy smile as we exit the building.

CHAPTER 11
Dani

"MAYBE WE CAN ORDER lunch for delivery," Michael says. "Just head home."

"Perfect," I respond, eager to be alone with them.

Until now, the pregnancy was more about the shock of it, morning sickness, pondering the future and all the logistics of how our lives are going to change. But seeing the ultrasound, seeing the baby move around inside me, has me in complete awe that is real and happening. I'm going to be a *mom*. To a lucky little baby who will have three incredible fathers.

I have these three men around me, supporting me, loving me, devoted to our relationship and our child.

It makes me feel intensely feminine and madly in love with my guys. The energy surrounding all of us is crackling with emotion and sexual tension. We obviously all want to be home, where they can strip me naked and share me, giving expression to what we're all feeling. Or maybe just cuddle or take a shower together, but I don't think it will stop at that. We're all feeling the intensity of our love right now and our favorite way to express that is with our hands, mouths, and being together in every way.

Michael is running a hand over my lower back as we enter the parking garage and his eyes are shining with love. Crew keeps giving me flirty grins. He looks like he can't believe we're actually having a baby.

And Nathan?

Nathan looks almost feral in his love.

He wants this baby so much.

He wants *me* so much.

The minute we're at our car, he presses me against it, giving me a demanding kiss.

"God, I just love you so fucking much," he murmurs. "You're amazing, Danielle."

"I love you, too." I lean into him, palms on his chest, breathing in his scent. Nathan always smells like expensive cologne. Like strength, power.

"You are light and love and life to me," he says, dragging his mouth along my jaw. "You brought me to life first, now you're giving us all another life." His hand drifts over my stomach, circling possessively. "I swear to God, the thought of it makes me hard every time I think about how you came into my life, lit it all up, *made* me open my mind to an even bigger idea of love and family than I ever imagined." He drags his mouth down my throat to the pulse point at the base. "And you just keep giving me more and more and more." Then he slides his hand around to my ass and brings me up against his hard body. "And it makes me want to tie you to my bed so I can take care of you, and never let anything or anyone ever hurt you, and fuck you constantly."

I'm breathing so hard, I can barely come up with words. I take his face between my hands. "Let's get home." Glancing over my shoulder, I notice our driver is absent. "Where's Andrew?" I'm disappointed we're going to have to wait for him before we can all be alone. I need to be naked with hands all over me and a cock inside me *now*.

"I texted him as we left the office to go get me a coffee and not to return for twenty minutes." Nathan steps back. "Get in the car."

Oh. I know that tone. Nathan isn't willing to wait. "We're in a parking garage!" My protest sounds weak even to my ears. My guys would never let anything happen to me. Even letting someone see me in an embarrassing situation.

"We have tinted windows."

Heat floods my inner thighs. "Nathan…"

He smacks my ass lightly. "Now, Danielle. I need to fuck you and you want this as much as I do."

He's right. I suck in a breath and step away so he can open the door of the backseat.

"You two can get in and watch or not," Nathan says to Crew and Michael without looking at them. "It's up to you." He presses his hand to the small of my back to urge me inside the car. "But our girl is riding my cock first."

Michael opens the passenger door and climbs in without hesitation. Crew hangs back. I give him a questioning look as I disappear into the rear interior. He leans in and gives me a grin. "I'll be on the lookout for Andrew. This will probably be the first time in Starbucks history there is no line. Besides, that's tight quarters."

Sometimes I'm still in awe at how lucky I am that my guys aren't jealous. Crew isn't staying out of the car because it would make him uncomfortable to see me having sex with just Nathan. He means what he says—he just thinks the backseat is too small for all of us.

And he might think it's kind of hot to only vaguely hear what's going on inside the car but have to wait until we're home to do anything about it.

"But," Crew adds. "Be a good girl and fuck him hard, Dani. A well-fucked Nathan is better for all of us."

I giggle. "Well, if I have to…"

Crew smacks my ass and then shuts the door.

Nathan has already gone around to the other side of the car. He's in the seat already undoing his belt and button. "Leggings off now," he commands.

I obey easily, swiftly. It always excites me when he gets like this—when he wants me so much his voice takes on a demanding edge. I lift my feet so I can pull the leggings off, but Michael reaches out from the front seat and eases the pants off over my ankles.

"Why thank you," I tell him with a grin. My hormones and emotions are all bubbling up, like the fizz in soda pop. I'm so happy, I can't keep it inside. Yes, I'm horny as hell but I'm feeling joyous too. And I love that these emotions can all mix together when I'm with my men.

"Happy to help," Michael says. His velvety voice is low and rough. He gives me a wink and wets his lips, then his gaze drops below my waist. "Is that pretty little pussy wet already?"

"Ye–" I start.

"Is our girl hot and wet, Armstrong?" Michael interrupts. "Is she ready to spread her legs right here in this parking garage? Greedy and needy as always for us?"

Got it. Michael knows I love when they talk about me like this. I can't explain it other than to say that the need in their voices, the way they talk about my body and what I do to them, feels different when they're talking *about* me instead of *to* me. I love both. But they get dirtier and sound hotter sometimes when they're talking to one another *about* me.

Nathan's hand slides between my thighs and buries his finger deep inside me. I moan, eyes drifting closed momentarily.

"So fucking wet." He eases in and out of me with a swift rhythm. "It's needy too, isn't it, Danielle? *Our* pussy is aching, isn't it? It needs filled up and fucked, doesn't it?"

"Yes," I moan. Every time he saws in and out of me, his thumb rubbing over my clit, I cry out in pleasure.

When my eyes open again, Nathan is watching me, studying my expression. "Fuck, you're gorgeous when you're like this."

I'm breathing fast. "I love how fast you guys can get me to the edge."

"How fast we get *you* to the edge? Look at what you do to me." He gestures to where he's freed his cock.

Without even thinking about it, I bend over and flick my

tongue over the tip of his shaft, wanting to make him feel the way he makes me feel. Nathan growls deep in his throat and his fingers tangle in my hair. "That's my greedy girl. You want my cock, don't you?"

"Yes." I run my tongue down the length of him. "Can I suck you?"

"No."

I pout, because Nathan actually loves it when I pout. I sit up, glancing at the front where Michael is watching us, jaw set. I want them both. Starting this in the car is hot, but definitely has its drawbacks.

Nathan takes my chin and directs my gaze to his. "You're going to ride my cock until you scream in this car. Understood?"

My stomach swoops. I flick my tongue over my lower lip. "Yes."

"Come here." Nathan pulls me onto his lap in one swift motion, his palms tightly gripping my waist.

I settle in on his thighs, knees on either side of him. The tip of his cock is pressing against my slit and I roll my hips, teasing us both with the hot, wet contact.

"You are so damn sexy."

Then he shifts and the full length of him is deep inside me. I relax down onto his thickness with a happy sigh. *"Nathan."*

He can say that he wants me to ride him all he wants, but we both know how this is going to go—he'll be fully in control. That's immediately obvious when he thrusts deeply up into my pussy, fingers tight on my flesh, holding me in place. His pushes are so powerful I have to grab onto his shoulders so I don't fall sideways and I'm immediately wracked with an orgasm that has me shuddering in pleasure. *Wow*.

"Oh my God," I cry out, then bite down on my lip, afraid I'm being too loud.

"No way," he says. "Let me hear you, pretty girl. No holding back."

My teeth fall away from my lip and I stare into his eyes as my body clings to his.

"I love you," I murmur. "Is that what you want to hear?"

"Tell me how much you love me, wife."

"I love you infinitely. With everything inside me."

Nathan thrusts harder, and I'm pistoning on him, pleasure spiraling tight again deep inside me.

"You love *me* inside you."

I nod, frantic now, desperate to come. Nathan raises his hand and teases at my nipple. With a hiss, I shatter again.

This time, he comes with me, until we're both panting and staring into each other's eyes, our bond unbreakable.

Until Crew raps on the window. "Incoming," he says. "Andrew at twelve o'clock."

"Jesus," Nathan mutters.

I laugh softly, slumping against him. "I can't move."

Nathan sets me aside as Michael passes back my leggings.

"That was hot as hell," he tells me. "And thanks to you I am now hard as a fucking rock." His gaze pins me. "The second we're through the front door, I want you bent over the couch. Understand?"

I nod.

"I can't hear you," Michael says.

I shiver. Michael is my sweet lover, but when he gets demanding it does delicious things to me. "I understand."

"Why the hell did you wear leggings?" Nathan demands as he attempts to slide them up my legs while I'm making fuck-me eyes at Michael.

I laugh and start tugging. He's bent over and tugging and swearing.

"This is your fault," I remind him.

"Nothing is ever my fault. It's always your fault for being so damn adorable," he grumbles from somewhere around my ankles.

We can hear Crew making small talk with Andrew and lying

to him that Nathan is on a business call. Michael is just shaking his head and fighting a smile.

Nathan finally emerges from between my legs. "I give up."

I lift my butt and yank the leggings up the rest of the way. "Funny how you never give up when it comes to taking my clothes *off*."

Somehow, he looks miraculously intact. His pants are slightly wrinkled, but otherwise you'd never know.

"I'm not complicated, pretty girl. I have simple needs, and all of them include you."

I melt a little at that.

He raps the window with his knuckles and Crew and Andrew join us in the car.

Crew gives me a knowing grin, his gaze raking over me. "The second we're through the front door–"

"Michael already called dibs," I say with what I'm sure is a naughty grin.

Crew leans in and captures my lips. "Shower after it is, then. Best for last."

"I heard that," Nathan says.

"So did I," Michael says.

"So did I," Andrew says with a chuckle. "I'm going to assume no one needs to make any stops on the way home."

"No," all four of us say at the same time.

CHAPTER 12
Nathan

"PRETTY?"

I nod. "Very pretty."

Gracie, Mark and Marissa's three-year-old, tips her head to the side and smiles at me. Obviously I gave the right answer. Fortunately for me, it's been the right answer the last three times she's asked.

She holds out a tiny hand, palm up. "More."

I know the game now. I open my wallet, extract a dollar bill, and lay it in her palm.

She gives me an even brighter smile and says, "Thank you."

I grin as I watch her head straight back to Danielle.

She hands Danielle the dollar then points at her head. "I want more pretty."

Danielle meets my gaze, her own smile bright and sunny.

She reaches into the tray of hair accessories she has set on the side table, extracts a sparkly pink bow with a clip and holds it up. "How about this one?"

Gracie shakes her head. "Gween."

It's the fourth time she's asked for green. I think the girl has a favorite color.

Danielle laughs softly, then takes a green barrette from the tray and holds it up. It's shaped like a heart. "This one?"

Gracie nods her head emphatically. "Yes."

Danielle gathers the little girl's silky hair into another little bunch that she pulls up and clips on top of her head with the three other green barrettes.

"You're *gorgeous*," she tells the little girl.

Gracie spins around so that Danielle can get the full picture, obviously. Then she leans in and squishes Danielle's face between her hands and says, "Gworgees."

I can see the delight in Danielle's eyes and I wonder which of them is having more fun.

Gracie spins and comes back to me.

"Pretty?" she asks me again.

I nod. "Even prettier," I tell her.

"More," she demands, holding her hand out again.

I laugh. I assume this means that she knows all about how going to the hair salon works because of visits she's taken with Marissa. I wonder though if Marissa gets away with simply holding her hand out to Mark and saying "more."

Probably.

It would work for Danielle.

And though Mark pretends to be put upon and run down by his beautiful younger wife and their little family, I know he's completely smitten with them all.

"More barrettes?" I ask Gracie. "Your head is almost full."

She shakes her head this time. "Cupcake!"

I glance up at Michael. He's standing behind the couch watching. He's got Gracie's baby brother up on his shoulder. Michael's hand cradles the tiny body as he pats the boy and sways, trying to get him to go to sleep.

He's been fussy ever since his mom and dad left though.

When Mark and Marissa mentioned on the fourth that they'd love to have a night out, Danielle and Michael practically tripped over one another offering to babysit anytime.

I have to admit that it's probably good practice for us.

I haven't been around kids much and certainly not infants, but I know Michael has. He has a number of nieces and nephews and he just exudes competent, confident 'Dad vibes'. That's what Crew calls it, anyway.

I know initially Hughes' calm composure in any situation was what drew Danielle to him—well, that and his eyes and mouth and brain and love of books and dirty talk.. believe me, she's gone on and on about all of that. But I'll admit now that the way Hughes is so hard to rattle is one of my favorite things about him, too.

But I was in on the babysitting because seeing Danielle with the baby at our party had made me soft and hard at the same time.

I felt as if my heart was melting in my chest and I could so easily imagine her holding our baby. She seems like a natural and I know our child will grow up believing his or her mother is the sweetest, most loving, supportive woman they've ever met. They'll worship her.

But it had caused a primal reaction as well. I'd thought my reactions to simply knowing she was pregnant, seeing her belly grow and her body change would be the end of it, but it seems every milestone that takes her closer to motherhood makes me want her more and more.

Right now, as I've been watching her fasten tiny plastic barrettes into the hair of a sweet little three-year-old, I want to throw Danielle over my shoulder, climb the stairs, throw her on the bed and fuck her senseless.

I wonder if this is ever going to go away.

I'm starting to understand why some families have so many children. Some of us men never quite got past our Neanderthal era.

"Cupcake!" Gracie demands, pulling me back to the moment.

I hand her another dollar. "See if Danielle has any cupcakes in her hair shop."

Gracie carries the money to Danielle. "Cupcake," she tells her.

Danielle pretends to get a cupcake out of the box of hair accessories. She holds her hand out. "Here you go," she tells Gracie with a smile.

But Gracie frowns and points at Danielle's hand. "Eat cupcake."

Danielle looks at me. "Uh oh."

I look at Michael. "Uh..."

"He better not have any—" She glances at Gracie then spells, "C-u-p-c-a-k-e-s in this house that I don't know about."

He taps her on top of her head. "I don't. And if I did, you and Crew would have cleaned them all out by now, just like you did the c-o-o-k-i-e-s Crew supposedly got for me and Nathan."

"I can't deprive your baby of the sweets he or she so obviously wants," she says, resting her hand on her belly.

Her words work exactly as she anticipated and Michael's little frown softens at the words 'your baby.' God, we're all so easy for her. We always have been but now that she's pregnant and wearing our rings, she can do absolutely no wrong.

"Well, something else," I say, lifting my shoulder. "Are you sure she even knows what a c-u-p-c-a-k-e is?"

Michael chuckles. "I am pretty sure she does. That's not a complicated concept."

"Well, what do we have?"

"Cupcake!" Gracie demands.

"We don't have any sweets at all," Michael says, lowering his voice as if Gracie won't be able to hear him. "Unless I make something."

"You should *totally* make something," Danielle says enthusiastically. She slides a sly look at Gracie, then says, "Like brownies."

"Bwownies!" Gracie parrots.

Michael gives Danielle a stern look. "That was naughty."

"Oh no," she says. "Brownies and a spanking, how terrible."

"Bwownies!" Gracie says again.

Michael growls and tugs on a strand of Danielle's hair. "Maybe no brownies for you and only for Gracie."

Danielle laughs and picks up her phone.

But Michael grabs it, balancing Romeo with one big hand. "And no calling Crew to bring you something."

She pouts up at him. "Please? I'll work off all the calories later…"

He looks over at me. "A little help here? Her sweet tooth is out of control."

I sit back and grin. "One, I love to help her burn calories. And two, whatever DNA is in there causing these cravings, it's not my fault."

Michael sighs. "You're right. And the way she's eating it probably *is* McNeill's kid."

Danielle just giggles at that and Michael grins at the sound. "Cookie, you are—"

"Cookie!" Gracie yells. "I want a cookie!"

I laugh out loud and pull my phone out. "Should I order something?" I've learned there's very little that my credit card and an app on my phone can't solve.

"Yeah, I guess," Michael says. "That should be faster than me making anything. But are we sure Gracie can have sweets? Did Marissa and Mark give us any instructions?"

"No, so I assume it's fine, right?" I ask. "If there was something she isn't supposed to have, they would've told us." I frown as I think about that. "Wouldn't they?"

"Maybe we should stick to something safer," Michael says. He focuses on the three-year-old.

"Gracie!" He makes his voice sound excited. "I have something in the kitchen to show you!"

She claps her little hands together. "Cupcake!"

Michael gives me a look. "Can you text Mark?"

"I guess I should." I start scrolling my phone for numbers.

But the little girl suddenly standing in front of me demands my attention.

"More!" She sticks her hand out.

"You need money?" I ask.

She nods. I give her two more dollars.

I glance up to find Danielle smirking at me. "What?" I ask.

"I just love how easy you are. I can totally picture our own kids someday just sticking their hands out and saying more and Daddy Nathan pulling out his wallet."

I shrug. "They'll be spoiled brats," I admit.

"No, they won't." Michael says firmly.

Danielle looks back-and-forth between us, her smile wide, but I can see that her eyes are watery.

"What's wrong?" I ask, leaning forward.

"Nothing. I just love how you both referred to our *kids* as they. As in plural."

Michael rests his hand on top of her hair, stroking softly. "You didn't think we were going to stop at just one, did you?"

She shakes her head. "No, probably not. But we haven't talked about it."

I wiggle my eyebrows at her. "Well, definitely one of the advantages of having a very young, insatiable wife is that we can knock her up several times."

She visibly shivers. "That should not be hot. I should be much more feminist than to love the idea of the three of you keeping me at home, pregnant constantly and raising your kids. While writing books about hot s-e-x."

I give her a knowing look. Our girl was an only child to older parents who sheltered her. She wants a big, boisterous, loving family. And she's got three men to help and plenty of money to support them. There's no reason we can't give her all of that.

"But it makes you hot, doesn't it?" I ask her.

She squeezes her thighs together, telling me everything I need to know, but she still admits, "It really does."

I see Michael's hand tighten on her hair, too. It's affecting him as well.

"Knock her up," Gracie murmurs under her breath, carefully folding the dollar I gave her up and putting it in her pocket.

My attention is pulled back to the three-year-old standing in front of me.

"Oops," I say.

Michael laughs. "That could've easily come from Mark. Marissa will blame him if she says it at home."

We all laugh. Mark and Marissa are fortunately very laid back. Well, Marissa isn't entirely laid back but she's a good neighbor and I think she would have a good sense of humor about this. She seems thrilled that Danielle is pregnant and that there might be a little one next-door close to Romeo's age. Besides, she married Mark, didn't she?

I hand Gracie another dollar, noting that I should enjoy the time when a little girl thinks a dollar is a lot. She takes it over to Michael and hands it to him.

"Cupcake."

Well, at least she's willing to pay for it. Michael takes it from her then gestures toward the kitchen. "Right this way, Madame."

Gracie burps then says, "Say excuse me when you burp."

Which makes me grin. The concept is there, the delivery not quite on point yet.

"Can I take the baby?" Danielle says, holding out her hands and wiggling her fingers.

Michael chuckles. "I've barely had him for ten minutes. You're a baby hog."

She grins. "I know. Lucky for me the guys I live with let me get away with everything."

He sighs. "It's true. Lucky for *me*, you're easy and always h-o-r-n-y because watching you with the kids makes me want to spread you out on the kitchen table and I intend to do that the second Mark and Marissa pick these kids up."

I know exactly what he means. Good thing both of them will be fine with me joining in on that spreading-her-out thing.

"When we have this huge, really comfortable couch?" Danielle teases, shooting me a look.

"Anywhere, anytime." Michael kisses the top of her head, hands her the baby, and heads into the kitchen with Gracie.

Danielle just stares after him for a long moment. I'm sure thinking about after the kids are picked up.

Romeo starts fussing though, interrupting her dirty daydream.

She brings him in close, cooing and nuzzling him up against her breasts.

But he's having none of it. He starts squawking.

"Oh, no, no. Everything's okay," she says to him softly.

Then from the kitchen we hear Gracie yell, "No!"

"These are special crackers, though," Michael tells Gracie.

"I want a cupcake!"

"Sweetie, we don't have any cupcakes," Michael says, trying to reason with the child.

I haven't been around kids much, but even I know that reasoning with a three-year-old is not going to end well.

"I'm ordering," I call out to Michael.

But I'm not sure if he can hear me because Gracie is now crying loudly.

"They're just crackers," Michael tells her. "They're good."

"*No!*"

Danielle's eyes are wide as she looks over at me. Romeo is either sympathetic to his sister's distress or he's getting even more irritated with the adults who can't give him what he wants either and he starts to outright cry.

"Oh, crap," Danielle says softly.

"Want me to try?" I ask.

I don't want to try, nor do I have any reason to think I'll be comforting to him at all, but I recognize that I should probably get used to holding a baby. And I hate seeing Danielle looking so worried.

She's already getting up from the couch.

I don't know what I have to offer. If the kid doesn't want to be up against soft, sweet breasts, I've got nothing better for him. Still, I take him into my arms and cradle him against my chest. I cup the back of his head with one hand, his butt with the other.

He quiets slightly, but he's still fussing. Danielle stands just looking at the two of us. She has a strange expression on her face.

"What are you thinking?"

"That you look really hot right now," she tells me.

"Really?" I like that.

"And how if someone had told me a year ago that I would be standing here watching Nathan Armstrong hold a baby, and that we would be married, expecting our own, and that it would turn out that you are one of the sweetest, most loving, best people I've ever met, I would've told them they were crazy." She steps closer and puts her hand against my cheek. "But you are. All of these things. You've made me so happy, Nathan."

"Danielle—" I have to clear my throat. "You are—"

Suddenly Romeo makes a very strange noise and then I am covered in warm, sticky baby puke.

Danielle actually jerks back, her hand flying up to her mouth.

She better not be about to laugh.

I shift the baby away from my chest and look down. I'm dressed casually since we're hanging out at home but I'm still not thrilled to have the gray T-shirt I'm wearing covered in regurgitated formula.

"Well that explains why he was so upset," she finally says.

I grimace. "Guess so."

Romeo has definitely quieted down now.

I stand and hand him over, then start for the stairs so I can clean up. "Be right back."

"I'll come with you and we can clean him up too."

I turn to look at her. "We can?"

"He's poopy too," she says, wrinkling her nose. "You can just take him in the shower with you."

I stop and lift a brow. "Are you getting in too?"

"I'll be there to help. But I should stay out of the shower with a towel so you can hand him back off."

"But you should probably be naked for that. You wouldn't want your clothes to get all wet."

She grins. "Are you starting to notice some other good things about having babies around?"

"It's not *not* a perk," I tell her.

There's another shriek from the kitchen. "No cheese!"

Dani looks at me with white eyes. "Wasn't this the kid who was eating cheese nonstop on the Fourth?"

"That's how I remember it," I agree.

Michael comes down the hallway from the kitchen, carrying a very unhappy Gracie.

She has tears streaked down her red cheeks and she is pouting better than anyone I've ever seen.

"I'm striking out with everything," Michael announces. "Gracie and I think that she needs some quiet time."

"No!" Gracie announces.

Dani is biting her bottom lip. I give her a look that says *do not smile*.

I'm sure she knows better. Michael is our rock. He is extremely difficult to shake. But I get the impression that over the next few years with our children, we may see Dr. Hughes actually reach his limit. He might even raise his voice.

"We don't yell, we don't throw food, and we don't spit cheese on the floor," Michael tells Gracie.

She simply opens her mouth and lets out a long, loud, "Aaahhhhh!"

"What is going on in here?"

We all turn to see that Crew has come through the front door.

"Babysitting," Michael says grimly.

"We don't have any c-u-p-c-a-k-e-s," I tell him.

"We still need more practice," Danielle adds.

Crew grins at us. "Good thing daddy three is home."

He tosses his workout bag to the side and then focuses on the little girl in Michael's arms.

"Hey Gracie, I was hoping I'd get to see you." He steps closer and holds out his arms. "Come here."

Gracie nearly launches herself at him, clearly desperate to get away from the very mean man who won't give her cupcakes.

"You're three?" she asks him.

He looks confused, then remembers calling himself daddy three. "Nope, I'm old. I'm Daddy Three. Our baby is going to have three daddies. One—" He points to me. "Two—" He points to Michael. "Three." He points to himself.

"Should we be... doing that?" I ask.

Crew shrugs. "Normalize it now. We're right next door. She's going to figure it out or ask eventually."

"Daddy three," Gracie repeats, patting Crew's chest.

"Yep. And it's always better to have three of something instead of just one," Crew says. "Just ask Dani." He gives Dani a wink.

I groan. "So now we'll be in trouble when she starts asking for another daddy because she's only got one?"

Crew shrugs. "Only with Mark. Marissa would probably be fine with that."

"Crew!" Danielle says, but she's grinning.

"Mark might be too," Michael muses. "He's mentioned how it's tough to keep up with a young wife and two kids. Maybe he needs a helper."

Crew nods. "Think of the shape poor Nathan would be in if he had to handle Dani all by himself. He'd never survive."

I shake my head. "Hilarious. I'm going to handle Dani upstairs right now. For the second time today."

"Hey, it's not break time," Michael protests.

Dani points at my shirt. "We have to clean him up. And Romeo."

Crew checks me out and grins. "Ah well, I can help you out, Boss. Give *Dani* a break."

I reach out and grab Dani's hand and start back up the stairs.

"If any other adults need to get naked during clean-up, I pick the hot redhead. You help the little princess there and save Doc."

Crew laughs and looks down at the little girl in his arms. She's got her head on his shoulder and she might be starting to drift off, actually. "I am starving. Do you want to play restaurant?"

She simply nods. Yeah, she's tired. Maybe she'll be asleep when Mark and Marissa get here and won't tell them about our failures tonight.

"Great. Let's go get some cheese," Crew tells Gracie.

I tense, waiting for her to yell.

But she says, "Cheese," as if that's the best idea anyone's had yet tonight.

I look back to see Michael rolling his eyes.

"Perfect," Crew says. "Doc? Do you want to be our first customer?"

"I'm really not in the mood for cheese," Michael says dryly.

"Oh, come on. Cheese is the best," Crew says. "Right, Gracie?"

"Cheese," the little girl agrees.

The three of them start down the hallway to the kitchen.

I look down at Danielle. She's watching them go with so much love in her eyes I can't help but lean over and kiss her.

"Crew's good," I say. "The kid whisperer."

"He is," she says affectionately. She looks up at me. "They really don't care whose baby this is, do they?"

I'm surprised she asked. I shake my head. "They really don't, Danielle. This baby is all of ours. In every way it matters."

Her hand goes to her stomach, cupping the bulge there. "I can't believe I ended up with you three. I have no idea how I got so lucky."

"Well, it has a lot to do with you being incredible and none of us being able to live without you."

She gives me one of the smiles that she'll occasionally shoot my way that absolutely steals my breath.

"I love you so much, Nathan."

"I love you too. And I love this life we have."

"I guess it's good that we're Cookie and Company. The company can just keep getting bigger," she says as we climb the stairs.

"I guess so. Or we could be Cookie, Company and a Macaron." I grin down at her. "Something sweet and small."

She shakes her head. "We can't use macarons. That's Luna's thing."

"What do you mean?"

"I can tell you. But it would mean you hearing about Luna's love life, or specifically her sex life."

"Never mind," I say quickly. "Cookie and Company it is."

CHAPTER 13
Michael

"I'VE GOT HER," I tell Nathan and Crew as I look down at Dani.

She's asleep on the couch, curled up with her head on a pillow, covered in a throw blanket Crew drew over her a little while ago.

"If you take her up to bed, we'll clean up down here," Crew says.

I scoop her up into my arms. Her eyelids flutter open. When she sees me, she gives me a sleepy smile and loops her arm around my neck. "Hi," she says softly.

"Let's go up to bed," I tell her.

"Okay." She rests her head on my shoulder. But as my foot hits the first step, her head pops up, her eyes wide. "Romeo! Gracie!"

"They're fine," I tell her, starting up the steps. "Marissa and Mark picked them up a little while ago."

"Oh, no," she groans. "I fell asleep while they were still here?"

"Yes. But so did the kids," I assure her as we hit the first landing.

"They must think I'm a horrible babysitter!"

"They definitely don't. The kids love you. Marissa and Mark love you. You were wonderful."

"I *fell asleep* in the middle of taking care of them!"

"Cookie, you're pregnant. You were tired. You knew the three of us were there taking care of things. You would never fall asleep if you were there alone with them." I keep climbing. Dani's light enough to carry, even while pregnant, but damn, I have to admit there are times when I agree with Nathan on the exorbitant number of stairs we have in this house.

Dani groans and drops her head back onto my shoulder. "I'm tired with two kids for just a few hours. And I had three people helping! I don't know how Marissa does it all the time. I don't know if I'm cut out for this."

I squeeze her tighter. "You are very cut out for this, Dani. You're going to be great. *We're* going to be great."

I know it's normal for an expectant mother to start to worry, but I will do everything in my power to assure Dani that she's going to be amazing. I've loved seeing her with our friends' kids. She's a natural. She's the most loving person I've ever met. She was meant to be a mom. My children—*our* children—will understand unconditional love from day one. It makes my heart swell. And other parts of my body swell.

I'm not as feral as Nathan is about Dani's pregnant body, but I'll admit there is something about her growing belly and seeing her mothering instincts kick in, that causes a very primal reaction in me.

"You have three very capable, very willing partners," I remind her. "You have nothing to worry about. Ever." I stop beside the bed and lay her down gently. I brace my hand on the mattress next to her. "We've always got your back. And this child will never want for anything." I brush the hair back from her face. "In fact, I am certain our child will wish for *less* attention at times."

She smiles up at me and lifts her hand to run it over my jaw. "That's another good reason for us to have several. Spread out all of the attention and intensity in this house."

I want that so fucking much, she has no idea. I would have a family of twelve with her and the guys.

I lean over and kiss her deeply, pouring my emotions into it.

When I lift my head, I pin her with a direct gaze. "I cannot wait to raise a family with you."

"Are you coming to bed with me?" she asks, skating her hand down my neck, over my shoulder and down my arm.

"Do you want someone in bed with you to fall asleep?"

There's more to do downstairs, but I know the guys are on top of it. I'm happy to cuddle our girl to sleep.

"Definitely," she says, sliding over to make room for me next to her.

The other side is Nathan's, of course.

I sometimes wonder, and grin, what Nathan's reaction will be when there's a toddler coming in during the night because of a nightmare and wanting to snuggle between Nathan and Dani.

Nathan doesn't like anything between him and Dani but I have a feeling that our little boy or girl will be an exception.

That makes my chest tighten. As much as I cannot wait to see Danielle as a mother, I'm also excited to see Nathan and Crew grow into fatherhood.

I know that we are very lucky to be in this position, the four of us doing this together.

"Okay, sit up," I tell her, tugging her into a sitting position so I can slip her dress off. She wears these long, loose dresses around the house now that her pants are getting a little tighter. She looks adorable with her rounding stomach in her fitting leggings and long shirts, but she says she likes the flow of the dresses.

Since the no-panties-at-home rule still applies, pregnant or not, she's naked as soon as I whisk the light flowery print over her head.

She lays back on the pillow, her hand resting on her stomach in what I think is a subconscious, protective pose.

I pull my shirt off and slip out of shoes, socks, and pants so that I'm down to only my boxers when I climb into bed next to her. She immediately turns to her side and tucks herself against me, her butt nestled against my pelvis. She pulls one of my arms over her and snuggles in against my chest, her head under my chin.

I love the feel of her in my arms. I love being able to bury my nose in her hair and inhale her scent. I love feeling her slowly drift off to sleep, her soft breath against my skin.

But we lay quietly for just a few minutes before her hand starts stroking over my arm and she wiggles her ass against my cock.

I'm not fully hard. I didn't come to bed with any expectations. But my girl's soft warm body is up against me so I'm not entirely relaxed either.

"Lay still," I tell her softly.

She takes my hand and lifts it until I'm cupping one of her breasts.

"Dani," I say low, warning.

"What?" She asks. "You don't want to?"

She knows very well I want to. I always want to. I will never, ever get tired of making love to this woman.

"You're tired," I remind her.

"Not that tired," she says. "Love me, Michael."

I groan. Our girl is a dirty talker, and she can be very demanding. That is always hot. But when she's soft and sweet and talks about making love, it gets to me just as much.

"You need your rest," I say, even as I squeeze her breast gently and run my thumb over the hardened tip.

She arches into my touch. "I can sleep after."

I chuckle softly, and nuzzle my face against her neck, placing a hot kiss there. "How about I just give you an orgasm?" I ask. "Just something to help you sleep?"

"No," she says, wiggling against me again. "I want you to fill me up."

I groan louder and squeeze her nipple.

"Yes, more."

My girl always gets what she wants.

I slide my hand down the front of her body. My hand skims over the slight swell of her belly and I pause, stroking back-and-forth for a moment. *Our baby.* It never fails to suck the air out of my lungs momentarily.

Then I continue down between her legs. I cup her pussy. "I can get you off, just like this," I tell her.

She lifts her top leg, hooking it over my thigh, widening the space between her thighs. "I know. But I want you inside me," she says breathlessly.

I circle her clit, eliciting another moan, then slip two fingers deep. "So wet already," I praise.

She nods, her silky hair brushing against my chin. "Harder. Deeper, Michael."

I fuck my fingers in and out of her a few times, winding her need tighter. But now I'm fully hard and obviously my girl needs some release.

I remove my hand so that I can get rid of my boxers. She protests with a little whimper.

I squeeze her ass. "Patience, greedy girl. You said you wanted my cock."

She breathes out. *"Yes."*

I shift behind her, freeing my cock from the silk boxers. Then I press against her, spooning her.

She lets out a happy sigh when she feels us skin on skin.

I cup her breast again and tweak her nipple. "You ready?"

"Yes," she says softly. "I need you."

I position my cock at her entrance, then grip her top thigh, opening her wider as I thrust forward.

I sink in easily and we both sigh.

"This is my favorite place on earth," I say against her hair.

"I love this position," she tells me. "I feel so safe. Your arms around me, you filling me up completely."

I clasp her tighter, curling my body around her as I thrust slowly.

"You're everything to me, Dani. You know that, right?"

"I love you so much, Michael," she responds.

I stroke her clit with my hand as I thrust from behind, my pace picking up. She grasps my thigh and presses back against me with each thrust.

I feel her inner muscles start to tighten around me after only a few minutes.

"That's my girl," I praise. "Are you going to come for me? Already? You gorgeous thing."

"Yes, I'm getting close," she pants.

"Give me your mouth."

She turns her face to me and I seal my mouth over hers and start fucking her faster.

Her sweet pussy starts to pulse around me, and I know she's on the edge. I circle my finger faster on her clit, pressing harder.

And then she pulls her mouth away from mine, so she can cry out my name. "Michael!"

Her pussy clamps down, and I let myself go, thrusting into her deep and hard. My climax hits, and I empty myself into her.

I hold her as the ripples continue through both of our bodies for a few moments after. I kiss her hair, her cheek, her neck, her shoulder.

She holds on tight to my arm, hugging me against her.

Finally, when we've floated back to earth, I pull out and go to the bathroom to clean up. I bring her a warm washcloth and clean her as well. When I re-join her in bed, I don't bother putting my boxers back on. I just pull her into my arms, again skin on skin, and tuck her against my chest and under my chin.

Right where she belongs.

"You're giving me my dream life, Cookie," I tell her softly. "Thank you."

She sighs happily. "You never have to thank me for this. I sometimes feel selfish for how great everything is. I'm so happy I sometimes can't believe it. We're so lucky."

I kiss her neck. "It's not luck, baby," I tell her. "We've *chosen* this. We've made it work. There are a million reasons and ways for it to fall apart, but the four of us have *decided* to make it work. Each of us looked at our lives and said 'yes' to this."

She's quiet for a moment, then she turns to her back and looks up at me. "You're absolutely right. I guess it feels like luck because once we made that decision it felt fast and easy. But we *are* choosing it, aren't we?"

"Every day. With every new obstacle and adventure," I say with a nod.

I see her eyes glisten and I frown. "Don't cry." I cup her cheek. "There's nothing to worry about. We're all here. We're all in."

She nods. "I know. It just hit me that it feels even bigger and *stronger* this way. The choosing. That's so much better than luck."

I smile and lean over to kiss her. "So, so much better," I say against her lips.

I hold her as she drifts off to sleep. And I study the rings on her left hand.

There needs to be a third, dammit.

Nathan and I need to have a talk with Crew.

Yes, we all need to make choices about how this relationship and family fit into our lives and our future but he's a part of this and we're not letting him go.

And it's probably time Nathan and I tell him that.

CHAPTER 14
Nathan

A YEAR AGO, if I'd been asked to attend a baby shower, I would have paid a million dollars to get out of it. I would have written that check and not thought twice about it, because a baby shower would have been the most obvious display of everything that I would never have—a wife, a child.

That was then.

This is now. And I have both. I have my Danielle, who is my spiritual and legal wife now, since we went down to the courthouse last week and stood before the judge. Then there is our baby, who is healthy and growing and going to be born into this world surrounded by love.

So I've bought out Danielle's favorite brunch restaurant for her baby shower and I'm standing here with a blood orange mimosa in my hand, eyeing the explosion of decorations that Lorraine, Lori, Luna, and Michael's sisters have spent the morning setting up and I'm thrilled to be here. I am also happy to pay for it all knowing we have the legalities worked out, papers drawn up by my lawyer to cover any and future scenarios for our family.

Now if I drop dead from a heart attack or from sheer annoyance with Crew, Danielle is protected. Crew saunters up to me and eyes the flute in my hand. "That doesn't look like Bourbon."

"When in Rome," I tell him, raising the glass.

"I don't understand the theme," Crew says, hands in his pockets. "Are oranges really that cute?"

Danielle requested we all wear our brunch best, which apparently means suits for us, and a skin-tight green dress to show off her tiny baby bump. I've been told by the women this is early in a pregnancy for a shower, but we wanted to do it before the hockey season starts, so the uncharacteristically tight dress is Dani's way of showing off her not-so-big-yet belly. She looks beautiful surrounded by all the peach and orange and green flowers and balloons, green eyes sparkling, cheeks bright with color. There are little oranges on everything from the banner to the table centerpieces to the menu cards with the phrase, "A little cutie is on the way," accompanying it.

"I guess. Tiny oranges are cute. I don't know." I haven't even thought about it, to be totally honest.

The majority of the guests haven't arrived yet. I decide I want to talk to Danielle before she's too busy receiving congratulations and gifts. But Michael appears beside us and hears the last bit of our conversation.

"Clementines," he says. "They call them 'cuties.' That's where the theme came from."

Of course Hughes knows that. And that makes more sense.

"Oh." Crew frowns a little, like he still doesn't entirely get it. "I would have thought it would be like a play on cookies or buns or something."

"Dani says she has to leave the pastry puns for Luna to use since she's a baker," Michael says.

Crew's mouth drops. "My sister is pregnant?"

"No, no. At least not that I've been told." Michael laughs. "For at some point in the future. It's a girl thing. Not stealing each other's themes and baby names."

Crew makes a sound of relief. "Good. I feel like it's too soon for Luna and those guys. They've only been together a few months."

That makes me snort. He doesn't even see the irony.

"And I can't believe Dani doesn't want to do a gender reveal and I can't believe that I decided to stand with her on this," Crew adds. "It's kind of driving me crazy and I don't even know why. I don't care if it's a girl or a boy, I just want a visual when I'm thinking about the future, you know what I mean?"

I nod. "Stay strong, McNeill. Dani will be disappointed if you cave." Easy for me to say since I know the sex of the baby. It allows me to take the ultrasound printout out of the safe where I had to put it so Dani and Crew wouldn't be tempted to dig it out of a drawer. I stare at it in awe at least once a day. I can't get over the tiny baby growing inside my wife.

Michael and I have looked at it together and discussed what we know that they don't know, but only when we're absolutely certain we won't be overheard. Danielle would be so disappointed if she found out before the birth, so we're keeping the secret.

"I know, I know. Boy or girl, this kid is getting skates for their first birthday. Got to keep the tradition alive."

"Agreed."

Danielle's mother has arrived and the minute she lays eyes on the three of us, we all tense. Danielle tends to defend her parents' behavior, and I know they're trying, but they still piss me off. The sour look on Mary's face as she racks her gaze over us leaves no doubt how she really feels about our family dynamic.

"Brr. It just got cold in here." Crew pretends to shiver, which is his usual reaction to Mary Larkin. It kills him that she's probably the only female in Illinois who doesn't think he's cute, charming, and sweet.

"You knew she'd be here," I remind him.

"Yeah, and I should remember that it's really *Doc's* fault that Mary's pissed off," Crew says.

"Me?" Michael asks. "What did I do?"

"You knocked her baby girl up."

Michael snorts. "Only because you were hurt. Otherwise, this could totally be your fault."

"You know," Crew says, watching Mary greet a few other guests, "even though she doesn't know the baby's yours, and the minute Mary sees him or her she'll forget all about being annoyed, I think I'm glad you went first." He claps Michael on the shoulder.

I chuckle.

"Chin up, she's coming over here," Michael murmurs.

"Hello, Nathan. Michael." Mary leans in to allow me to air kiss her cheek.

"Mary. Thank you for coming."

Michael gives her a loose hug.

Then she turns to Crew, who has a smile plastered on his face. It also bothers him that Mary doesn't take him seriously as a part of Danielle's life. "Mary. Great to see you."

"I'm surprised to see you here," she tells him.

That makes me tense even more. I draw myself up straighter and I see Michael's posture change from relaxed to alert. Crew's smile grows strained.

"Why is that?" Crew asks. "Dani *is* having *our* baby."

Her brow furrows. "Oh, so you know who the baby belongs to? I just assumed it wasn't yours since you and Dani aren't married."

I don't follow that logic at all. I'm pretty sure Mary knows Crew and Danielle are sleeping together, despite the wedding situation. But Mary doesn't have much of a sense of humor and I also don't want to get into a detailed discussion of my infertility and our group sex life with her, so I just keep my mouth shut. In fact, I clench my jaw tightly.

"The baby is *ours*," Crew says. He points to me and Michael. "All of ours."

"Well, that's not really true, is it?" Mary says, rolling her eyes. "And you and Michael travel all the time. My daughter is going to be raising this baby alone half of the time. I really wish she would have waited to start a family."

"Nathan will be here with her when Michael and I are out of

town. And *we* are all thrilled to be starting a family now," Crew says. "This baby is very welcome." There's an uncharacteristic bite to his voice.

Mary doesn't look convinced.

It makes me feel bad for Crew. I've done this too—underestimated him, written him off as too young or immature, steamrolled over his wants. But he's a grown man, and he's made the decision to be all in on this family and I admire him for that. I'm also grateful for him. He adds something to our mix that we all need. He also makes my wife very, very happy. And he's going to be a wonderful father.

Michael clears his throat. "When it comes to love and support and resources– time, energy, money and everything else–the baby has three fathers, Mary. Everyone needs to understand that."

Michael's deep, calm voice, not surprisingly, seems to work. Mary's frown relaxes.

Crew shoots him a grateful look and I feel the tension in my shoulders loosen.

Fuck, we are so lucky to have Hughes. Our family, with our unconventional arrangement as well as my and McNeill's big personalities, needs him.

Mary swallows, then nods. "Well, I do appreciate that."

"Your *grandchild* will have so much love, and support, Mary," I promise her, making sure she can see my sincerity, along with my reminder that she's going to be a grandma and she should be happy about that, dammit. I could launch into an entire monologue about how much I wish my grandfather could understand all of this and how much he would love this baby and that she should be *grateful* to be a part of this.

She meets my gaze directly, which I admire. "I just want Danielle to be happy."

"Mary." Crew waits until she looks back at him. "Danielle's happiness is *the* most important thing to me in this entire world. And I understand that it might take you some time to truly believe that. But I'm not going anywhere. So that means that in five years, or ten years, or twenty years, however long it takes, you *will* understand how much your daughter and *all* of your grandchildren mean to me, and even if you never say it, I will know that you know. It will be impossible not to believe it."

Damn.

I lift a brow and meet Michael's gaze.

He looks impressed, too. And doesn't say another word. He just claps Crew on the shoulder. So I do the same.

I look at Mary.

She's staring at Crew.

He simply holds her gaze. He doesn't look angry or aggressive. He just looks like a man who has said his truth and is confident with whatever happens next.

Finally, Mary takes a deep breath. Then she says, "Okay."

I fight a smile. That's about as good as we're going to get from her right now.

But I think Crew's right. Someday she'll really know it. And we'll all know that she knows.

"Try the shrimp, Mary," I say, taking her by the elbow and steering her toward the buffet. "It was flown in fresh this morning. Would you like a mimosa?"

"I need something a lot stronger than that," she says, in a candid statement that almost makes me grin.

"We can do that." I understand why she and Danielle's father are struggling with our relationship. But that's their own shit and I won't enable it in any way. I absolutely hate that it robs Danielle of some of her joy during these milestones of our lives together. I want to tell Mary exactly how I feel about what she's doing to her daughter, but I won't ruin today for Danielle. It's her moment, not Mary's.

But I can't stop myself from saying, "It doesn't matter if you understand any of this, but you need to let Danielle be happy today."

"I do want that, Nathan."

In the life she envisioned for her, not the one Danielle has chosen.

Before I say any of what I'm thinking, Lori McNeill meets us, gives me a smile, and links her arm through Mary's. Lori turns Mary away from me, launching into an explanation of the massive buffet that is covering three tables. I'm going to buy that woman a very expensive piece of jewelry for her birthday, or Mother's Day, or…next Wednesday. Lori McNeill can talk to a tree stump and I've never appreciated that more than I do now.

More guests are arriving. Val gives me a hug and Marissa comes in with Romeo in tow. She's left Gracie with Mark, which is probably a good thing. The buffet is light on cheese. I recognize Michael's sister-in-law, Crew's aunt and Elise from Books and Buns.

Before I lose the opportunity to talk to our girl, I slide up behind her and wrap my arm around her waist, resting my palm on her bump. "Is this what you pictured?" I murmur in her ear.

"Yes." She glances up at me. "It's perfect, thank you."

"Thank Lori and Lorraine. They did the heavy lifting. Can I get you anything?"

She shakes her head. "I'm fine right now."

The gift table is rapidly filling up and I see several people coming over to speak to her. I kiss the side of her head and step forward to get swept into a hug by Crew's aunt. The McNeills are a touchy-feely family.

For the next hour, I just circle the room as the women all chat and sit down to eat. Michael is sitting with his mother and sisters and Crew is eating off of a plate as he walks around checking in with people. I'm not eating. I'm just soaking it all in. Everything I've gained. It feels incredible and my throat is too damn tight to swallow any food.

When it comes time to open gifts, Luna and Lori are like a well-oiled machine, handing gifts to Danielle before whisking them away and creating some elaborate display of them. I'm not even sure what I'm looking at there is so much baby gear. Apparently, anything less than forty onesies is inadequate.

"Are you ready for all this?" Val asks me, coming up beside me and handing me a plate of food and a fork. "You need to eat."

"Thanks." I absently scoop up some of the black truffle risotto. "This is really good."

"You didn't answer my question."

"I'm eating. You told me to eat." I swallow the risotto. "But yes, I'm ready. I can't wait, actually."

"Even for three in the morning feedings?"

"Danielle is going to breastfeed." I give her a smile. "But I will get up and help her change and settle the baby. I'm ready, willing, and able to do anything."

"I'm buying you all one of those bears with the camera in it," Val declares. "I want to see that."

"You don't believe it will happen?" I ask the woman who was as much a mother-figure as anyone in my life.

She faces me fully and gives me a soft smile. "Actually, I do believe it will happen. And I really want to see it because seeing you that happy will be so amazing to witness, Nathan."

I don't know what to say. I swallow hard. "Thank you, Val."

"And I will be insisting on babysitting. Getting rid of *four* doting parents will be a challenge, I realize, but I *will* be getting my baby fix, understand?"

I grin, grateful that she knows me well enough to let me off the emotional hook. I lean over and kiss her cheek. "I understand."

She pats my cheek. "You really do. Finally."

And I know she's not talking about her insistence on babysitting.

I have always thought my purpose was to take the Racketeers to a championship win. What I realize now is that's a goal—my *purpose* is to love my wife and build a family with her.

It's the most important thing in my life.

Sometimes that also means letting my wife handle things her way, which is tested an hour later when most of the guests have left and I see her in the back of the restaurant having a heated conversation with her mother. I'm about to storm back there and intervene when Crew grabs my arm.

I glance over at him. "What?"

He shakes his head. "Let her handle this, Boss."

Michael is behind him. He nods. "He's right."

"But that doesn't mean we can't get closer and listen in case we do need to put Mary in her place," Crew says, swiping a macaron on his way past the dessert table. He gives me a smirk as he shifts closer to where Dani is standing.

"You're being obvious," I tell him, dryly.

"That's the point. Show of strength."

I glance back at Michael. He just shrugs. "We have to load all the gifts into the car anyway," he says. "They're standing right by the gift table."

He has a good point. I reach the gifts and finger a pack of the tiniest socks I've ever seen in my entire life. There's going to be tiny feet in these socks. My heart is so damn full I almost can't take it.

"Mom, I appreciate you being here," Danielle is saying to Mary. "But I don't want you to come to important events in my life if you're not actually happy for me."

"I'm happy you're happy," Mary says tightly.

"But you're not happy *for* me. That's very clear. I'm having a baby, Mom. A *child*. Who is going to pick up on all your cues and passive aggressive comments and judgment about my life and my relationships. I will not expose my child to that. Crew, Nathan, and Michael are my child's *fathers*. I will not allow you to disparage them in any way. Not anymore. Not in front of our child, not in front of anyone. Because if I allow you to do that it implies that in some way I think we are doing something wrong, and we're not."

I glance over again. Danielle doesn't look angry or overly upset. She's just being firm, determined. Setting boundaries that

I'm thrilled with. I make eye contact with Crew. He gives a nod of approval.

She keeps speaking. "You're allowed to have your opinion. You're allowed to disapprove. But not around me, and absolutely not around my child. So you have a decision to make. You're either with me, fully and sincerely, or you're not in my life. Period."

Michael gives a little grunt of approval.

I smile back at him. "Our wife has found her inner mama bear defending her cub."

"I don't think anything could be sexier," Michael says. "This needed to happen. I just hope her mom makes the right choice."

"She will," Crew says. "Who could possibly live without our girl?"

"None of us, that's for damn sure."

He laughs. "No fucking way."

Mary is hugging Danielle with tears in her eyes so that seems promising, though I can't hear what she's murmuring in her ear.

A moment later, Mary moves past us. She squeezes my arm, pats Michael on the shoulder, and shocks us all by pulling Crew into her arms and giving him a hug, tears rolling down her face.

"You'll be a wonderful father," she tells him, her words tight and low.

Then she quickly heads to the front of the restaurant and leaves. We all stare at her retreat, then immediately turn to Danielle.

"Are you okay?" Michael asks her immediately.

She nods. "Completely. I should have done that before the wedding. But I did it now, so we'll see how it goes. She says she'll do better."

Crew cups her cheek and kisses her. "Good girl."

"I'm proud of you," I tell her.

"I know that was hard for you, Cookie," Michael says. He runs his hand down her bare arm. "But you were fierce."

"And sexy as fuck," Crew tells her.

She smiles. "Yeah? It felt…powerful."

"You were magnificent," I tell her.

Her smile is bright and confident.

"Now let's get the car loaded," Michael says. "It's going to be fun unpacking all this at home."

I give an exaggerated groan. "We have to carry this stuff up all those stairs? Can't wait for that."

Danielle gives me a soft kiss. "Wait until you're carrying a baby up and down those steps."

"Now *that* I can't wait for."

I really can't.

This baby can't come soon enough for me.

"When we get home, I might need a nap," Danielle says. She gives me a flirty look as she picks up the absolute smallest package possible on the table and saunters past me. "Naked."

"I am definitely a nap guy," Michael says.

Which is not true at all, but we all know Danielle isn't talking about sleep.

"I've got this one covered if you get too worn out on the stairs, Boss," Crew says, clapping me on the shoulder.

I lift the biggest box on the table. "You wish."

CHAPTER 15
Crew

I STRETCH out on the couch with a loud, long, very contented sigh. I make sure my legs and arms all stretch as far as they possibly can.

"Okay, Okay," Nathan says.

I smirk at him.

"I don't think you have any idea how much I love the fact that you bought a couch exactly like the one you got rid of."

"I don't want to talk about it."

Nathan is propped on the other end of the couch. The exact replica of the ginormous couch we owned for a few months that he bitched about constantly, and that he got rid of because he insisted it was a hazard to our soon-to-be born child.

He proceeded to buy, have delivered, and then sit on three different couches for two days each.

He hated them all. They were too small, too hard, or both.

It was like watching fucking Goldilocks try the three bears' beds and I enjoyed every second.

So one day while we were all gone, he ordered this couch. Which is exactly like the one he got rid of.

I walked in the house that day, saw the thing taking up most of the space in our living room and almost cried.

I love this couch so much.

I also love the fact that Nathan said he tried to get the old couch back from the dude who bought it from us, but the guy loved it and wouldn't sell it back. Not even for more than he'd paid for it. So Nathan had to buy this one brand new.

"I will get rid of it again just to shut you up," Nathan says.

I laugh. He won't. He tried three other couches and couldn't find one he liked.

"No," I say. "You're stuck with this couch just like you're stuck with me."

I take a huge handful of cheese popcorn and throw it up in the air, catching it in my mouth.

Well, I catch most of it. Two kernels bounce off my chin and onto the couch cushions.

"Dammit McNeill," Michael grouses from his spot on the couch between Nathan and I.

"No big deal," I say. "Nathan said he got it stain-treated. We're going to have a little kid around here. You don't think there's gonna be worse things on this couch than cheese popcorn?"

"It's true," Nathan agrees. "Cheese popcorn is nothing."

"We can just have a no food in the living room rule," Hughes says. He narrows his eyes at me. "For everyone."

"No food for movie nights?" I protest. "Cruel and unusual punishment." I toss more popcorn into my mouth. "When it gets bad enough, Daddy Nathan will just buy us another couch."

Both Doc and I look at Nathan. He just shrugs.

"Fuck, I love Daddy Nathan," I say. "I want a white pony, please."

"I suppose the pony will get to be on the couch too?" Michael asks dryly.

I laugh.

It cracks me up that Nathan is actually the more laid back one about things right now. He is openly admitting that he intends to spoil our child. While Michael is the one insisting we need rules and guidelines, and that we all need to agree that we're going to discipline the child similarly. He goes on and on about how sending the kid mixed signals will be unfair to him or her, and that if we have rules, we all have to enforce them.

It's also funny to me that Michael's more concerned about me and Nathan being too permissive than me and Dani being the easy-going parents.

Danielle has taken on this new air lately. She's become more serious, more protective, and stronger. More sure of herself. Yes, she's still sneaking junk food behind Michael's back—though we all know that he knows—and she worries that she's not ready to be a mom, but she's incredibly protective of the baby even still months from delivery.

She's put up boundaries with her mom and dad, she's been very strict about her sleep schedule, she's been doing yoga on a regular basis and, much to my chagrin, it's not always naked yoga with me.

And she is fully on board with Michael, and all of the rules and guidelines he wants to put in place.

Mama Dani is a pleasant surprise. And strangely sexy.

All through my life I have found rules and regulations something to be tested and pushed.

I don't think I'm gonna do that with Dani.

For one, I totally respect it. It's not just sexy, it makes me see her in a whole new light.

Plus, if she decides to discipline me it could mean cutting me off from sexy times and we all know that's the one thing that might actually work to straighten me up.

Danielle is probably the only person on the planet who can actually get me to behave.

"So hey, Crew, we want to talk to you about something," Nathan says.

I turn the volume down on the game on TV. "Actually I've got something, too. Something I need to discuss before Dani gets home."

Dani's at Books and Buns helping Luna train the new bookstore manager. This is the perfect time for me to get the guys' help with my plan.

"Yeah, we need to have this conversation before she gets home, too," Michael says.

"Okay," I say. "Let me go first. Mine won't take long." I need their help in planning something great, but I have a good idea and I just need their help making it happen.

"Ours is pretty important," Nathan says, sitting up straighter on the couch. "Let us go first."

I frown and set the bowl of popcorn down. "Mine's serious. We don't know when she'll be home and I really don't want to put it off."

"Same here," Michael says, sitting forward and bracing his forearms on his thighs. "We really need to talk about this."

"I'm going to propose."

"You need to propose."

Nathan and I speak at the same time. We look at each other. Then I look at Michael.

"That's what you wanna talk about?" I look at Nathan. "You wanna talk about me proposing?"

"You want to propose?" Nathan asks.

"Of course I do. That's what I want to talk about. I have a plan and everything. But I need you guys to help."

Michael grins. "Thank God."

"Please tell me you're not surprised," I tell him.

"Not surprised. Just happy you're ready," he says.

"But you guys weren't sure and were going to tell me I needed to propose?" I should maybe feel like they're pushing or interfering. But that's not how this feels. I feel a warmth in my chest.

"It's time," Nathan says. "We gave you space, we let you think it through. But it's obvious you want to be here. We're family. You're not going anywhere. You need to give Danielle that commitment. You know she wants it."

"And it's kind of starting to piss us off that you are not willing to marry our wife," Michael says. "We want her happiness more than anything and that includes your ring on her finger." Michael pauses after that, seems to think about what he said, looks at both of us and grins. "Well, that sounded fucking weird."

Both Nathan and I grin.

"The thing is," I say. "It didn't really sound weird."

Nathan nods, then blows out a breath. "It didn't. McNeill, we want you to marry our wife."

I chuckle. "Well, I really want to fucking marry your wife, so I guess that's good."

Nathan shakes his head. "And to think a few months ago I was going crazy in my office thinking about either of you even taking her to dinner."

I agree. "We've all come a long way. I want to be a husband and a father. You've come around to having an entire family and sharing not just a house and couch, but everything. And Hughes..." I look over at Michael. "Actually, you're pretty much the same."

Nathan nods. "Of course he is. He's our rock. He's always gonna be the same. Thank God."

Michael chuckles softly. "Maybe in a lot of ways, but I've changed too. I always thought I knew exactly what my future looked like. Traditional. The wife, and kids, house, a dog. Never would've expected you two." He looks at us both with warmth in his eyes. "But this is even better than anything I imagined."

"Fuck yeah it is," Nathan agrees.

I pull in a long breath. "So, because I made her wait, I'm thinking I need to do a really huge grand gesture proposal."

Nathan rolls his eyes. "It has nothing to do with you making her wait. Of course you think you need to do a huge, over-the-top, crazy-ass proposal. That's just you."

Well, he's got a point.

Michael nods. "If you didn't propose in some crazy way, Dani would think something was wrong."

I grin. "Well then it won't surprise you to know that I already have an idea."

Nathan visibly braces himself. "Okay, lay it on us."

I look from one to the other. "I just have two words for you: Kiss. Cam."

CHAPTER 16
Crew

DANI IS FLOATING on her back in the pool at my parents' house, her belly popping up above the water. Her auburn hair flows around her, sunglasses on. She gives a happy sigh. "This is heaven right now. I am so hot."

"You are so hot," I tell her, eyes drawn to her bikini top. God, her tits look gorgeous right now.

Something about my voice gives me away, because she gives me a quick look of censure. "Behave. We're with your family."

"Oh, like being around family has ever stopped us before? I have one word for you—RV."

She giggles. "I think that's technically two words. Recreational vehicle."

"Whatever. That RV was rocking in your parent's driveway last Christmas."

Her cheeks turn pink from more than the sun. "Hmm. That was a special occasion."

"Every day with you is a special occasion."

Dani straightens up in the water and pulls her sunglasses down. "You're being very charming."

It's August and she's right, it is hot as hell. We're enjoying a leisurely Friday before having a big event at the arena the next day for charity. It's been a fantastic summer, filled with family and friends and watching Dani's pregnancy progress. I've been working out as usual and working with a specialized power skating coach. I've also let Dani talk me into doing morning meditations and yoga, which I jumped at because I thought it was code for morning sex but we've actually been following an app and getting our namaste on so she's ready for labor and delivery. A side benefit I didn't expect is it's quieted my head space a little and made my focus stronger because we go back for training in a month. I think that's going to be awesome on the ice and off moving forward.

Apparently, it's also made me charming.

I wrap my arms around her and give her a kiss. "Do you need some water? Gotta hydrate."

"That would be great."

"Be right back."

I launch out of the pool in one smooth leap, which has the added benefit of splashing Nathan, who is stretched out on a lounge chair like he's king of the suburbs, feet crossed, expensive sunglasses on, Rolex still on his wrist. There's a sweating glass of Bourbon on the rocks sitting on a table next to him.

"Hey, watch it," he says, not even opening his eyes.

I shake my hair over his legs, water droplets falling on his shins. "It's refreshing."

"Fuck off."

He sounds half-asleep. I take pity on him and leave him alone to take his old man nap. I head over to the outdoor kitchen by the back door and pull open the refrigerator door. Grabbing two bottles of water I kick the door shut again with my foot. Michael comes out of the house in his swim trunks and a T-shirt, wearing flip-flops and carrying a platter of vegetables and accompanying dips. My mother is right behind him, with a much more exciting platter of nachos.

"Need any help?" I ask.

My mother gives me a look. "You wait until we're carrying the food outside to ask that? No, we're good."

I shrug with a grin. "I was putting sunscreen on Dani."

My mother gives me a look. "If I had a free hand I'd put it up and say stop right there. Too much information, Crew."

She's probably right. I had spent extra time making sure I got every surface on Dani's body covered and massaged places that didn't even need sunscreen in my old teenage bedroom. Dani likes to change in there because it has a private bathroom and the added amusement of a peek into my hockey consumed adolescent mind. All my trophies and ribbons are still on display, plus an absurd amount of game pucks and old sticks. It still faintly smells like rubber in there even though I moved out five years ago.

"Let me take that, Mom." I start to set the water bottles down but she shoos me off.

"Go give Dani that water. I swear, it's like Satan sat his ass down on Chicago this week. I have the thermostat set at sixty and I'm still sweating." She places the nachos on the outdoor dining table. "I can't handle this heat. Menopause has me ready to internally combust. And your father wants to be all up on top of me in bed and I can't stand it."

I love that my parents still love each other, but her inability to see the irony also amuses me. "Mom. That also falls under the category of too much information."

Before she can respond, I take the water to Dani, untwisting the cap for her. "Here, baby, make sure you drink some of this."

She takes an obligatory sip and then sets it down on the pool deck. "Are you getting back in?"

"No, I'm going to eat. Are you hungry?"

"Not yet. I want five more minutes in the water. It's helping my back. I don't know how I'm going to do this for four more months."

"You're doing amazing." She is. She's working hard on her book and handling all the changes both to her body and to our household with ease.

Nathan has gone full control freak, buying everything under the sun for this baby. He's even given his private bedroom space for the baby's nursery. Which is great, except there are boxes arriving daily and a revolving door of delivery people carrying furniture up the stairs.

"It's probably because you're in a chair all day writing on the computer. You need to take breaks."

She smiles at me, kicking her feet behind her. "I will."

"If you don't, you will get spanked."

That just makes her smile wider.

I shake my head, amused, and head to the dining table, which is under an overhang and blissfully in the shade. My mother is right about the heat. I'm sweating my balls off. I settle down into a chair across from her and tuck into the nachos. "Where did Doc go?"

"He's back in the kitchen prepping the chicken for the grill. I love that you have him around to feed you. Left on your own you'd eat straight garbage."

"That is true. Where's Dad?" Luna and her boyfriends should be here soon. I'm looking forward to catching up with all of them.

"He's taking a cold shower."

That makes me laugh out loud.

"What?" my mother asks, sounding bewildered as she fans herself with a battery-operated handheld mister.

"Give the guy a break. He's not dead yet, Mom."

Realization dawns on her. She makes a face. "Oh, stop. He's just overheated from doing yard work. Which was absurd considering how hot it is today."

"He loves his yard. He and Michael have that in common."

My mother eyes me. "How are you?" she asks.

It's not a simple question. It sounds very leading. "What do you mean? I'm great."

I am. I think that's pretty obvious to anyone who knows and loves me.

"I know losing the championship was disappointing."

"Yes, it was. But I still have years of good hockey in me. I can't hang onto my disappointment." I pick another nacho up and put the entire thing in my mouth. I take a lot of shit for my eating habits, but I need a lot of calories. I'm constantly active.

"How about your relationship? Is everything good there?"

That makes me frown. I don't know if she's just doing a mom check-in or if she has some kind of agenda. "It's great, too. Why?"

My mom shrugs and gives me a gentle smile. "I just want to make sure that you're doing what *you* want. That you're not getting swept along with the crowd."

"You're calling Nathan and Michael the crowd?" I ask, amused.

"Well, Dani too. It's okay if you're not ready for all of this, Crew. You're a lot younger than them. You have to do what's right for you. Especially if the baby isn't yours."

I told my mother I thought it was more likely Michael is the biological father because of the timing of my injury simply because I didn't want her to somehow be disappointed if we find out it's not mine. I was trying to get ahead of it. I know my parents will treat any child I consider mine as a grandchild, but I still wanted them to at least be prepared so they could manage their emotions. Now I'm regretting saying anything because my own mother is hinting I can bail on my relationship.

"You know that Dani will be okay, right? Better than okay. Nathan and Michael are wonderful and they'll be there for her. She'll always have anything and everything she needs. You don't *have* to stay. I know you love her, but you don't have to stay out of guilt or because you feel like she needs you."

I watch my mother as she speaks. She seems uncomfortable which is interesting.

I should be the uncomfortable one. She's basically telling me I can leave Dani. That everyone would be fine. But I frown as my mom shifts on her chair and won't meet my eyes.

"Mom," I say, reaching out and grabbing her hand. "What is going on? What the hell are you talking about?"

She sighs. "I have to give you this. No one else will say it."

"Say what?"

She does meet my eyes now. She squeezes my hand. "That you don't have to stay. That you're a wonderful man and we know you love Dani, but that this all got really big and serious really fast and we would all understand if you changed your mind."

My eyes widen. I don't know how to feel about this other than shocked. "You would be okay with that?"

She shrugs. "We'd be sad. We love Dani and Nathan and Michael. We're excited about the baby. We want a family for you, if that's what *you* want and only when you're ready. We support *you*. Whatever you decide. I want you to know that. I don't want you to feel like you got…stuck."

I study her face. This is my mother. No matter how happy she is about the baby, no matter how much she adores Dani and the guys, she's *my* mom and she's giving me her unconditional support.

That's amazing.

And misplaced. And I need to let her know that so she can be fully happy and embrace everything that's happening. I feel bad that my family has had some doubts and haven't fully let themselves get caught up because they weren't sure of *me*.

In that moment, I'm one-thousand percent sure of all of it.

All of *us*.

"Mom. I love you. I love that you're concerned about me. And I'm so sorry I haven't made it crystal clear to *everyone* that I'm in. One-hundred percent. These are my people. This is my child. I know everyone is a little confused because I wasn't ready to get married, and hell, I confused myself a little. It was all fast and maybe I did feel like I was getting swept along. I needed to stop and take a breath, focus on the playoffs, then really figure out where my head and heart were. What I figured out is that there is no world I want to live in that doesn't include Danielle, Nathan, and Michael." My throat feels tight and I've crumpled a napkin into a little ball. "I choose them. Every day I will be choosing them." I take a breath. "I can picture a future without hockey but I can't picture a future without them."

She nods slowly, the corner of her mouth turning up. "Good," she says, softly. "I just wanted to make sure. You're going to be an amazing father."

Without warning, there are tears in my eyes. "I want this baby so much."

"Oh, Crew." Her other hand covers mine. "I'm so proud of you."

"I'm going to propose to Dani. The timing feels right now."

Her eyes widen. "Do the guys know?"

"Yes. They're helping me plan it."

She shoves her chair back and comes over to me. I stand up and let her hug me tightly. I hug her back. "I love you, Mom."

"I love you, too, sweetheart. This is wonderful news. Now I will officially have another daughter and two more sons, plus a grandbaby. Our family just keeps getting bigger and bigger."

On cue, Luna and Alexsei come through the back gate from the driveway, Coach Phillips and Cam hot on their heels. Luna has a giant floppy hat on and sunglasses. "The party is here!" my sister declares.

In my opinion, the party has already started.

Cookie & Co.

CHAPTER 17
Sammy the Malamute
(WADE)

I'VE ALWAYS VIBED with the Feeling Pucky event because it's for charity. This is my third one and I'm psyched.

Annually, all of the mascots in the league get together for a shooting competition. Okay, it's not *actually* a competition. The nets are attended by area kids who are coached by the goalies from all the teams. The players and fans divide up into "teams" for the various charities.

It's all about community and raising money for great causes and fun.

But the mascots make it into a competition. The traveling trophy is ugly as fuck and we play for it as if it's made of diamonds and gold. It's worth a year of bragging rights, and there's plenty of trash talk on the ice.

I don't really get into all of that. I'm just here to have fun. But I know everyone is always surprised that I'm a fantastic skater and have a really great slap shot.

Despite the Racketeers' loss in the championship, spirits are high in the arena tonight and the fans seem into everything. I'm feeling good, not only because I have a real chance at the trophy—I think Mr. Armstrong might get a kick out of me winning that on behalf of the Racketeers—but because Crew McNeill has a plan for tonight that will make the event especially memorable for our fans. And I get to be part of it.

First, I have to beat the damn dragon from Dallas, though. It's down to just the two of us.

I don't know who the fuck is wearing that dragon costume, but whoever it is keeps body checking me whenever he comes out onto the ice to take his position. He's trying to score on Blake Wilder and the kid he's coaching at the net.

I would probably know who this asshole is if I paid attention to the mascots' group chat. I'm in it, but I don't really participate. I'm going to find out afterwards when we all change out of our costumes, though. I don't know what this guy's problem is.

Still, I make a show for the fans, staggering backwards and windmilling my arms when he bumps into me. Then I pretend to get up in his face. The way he bumps into me feels pretty damned real though.

"What's your problem?" I ask low enough that the microphones around us won't pick it up. "Take it down a notch, huh?"

The dragon just shrugs and skates into position for his next shot.

I take a second to glance up into the stands. I love watching our fans react and interact with one another and the mascots and players.

Tonight, our players—other than the goalies—are up in the seats with the fans, supporting the mascots. The Racketeers are not all cheering for me. They're seated based on which charity they're "cheering for", but overall it's a fun change.

I locate McNeill sitting with his pregnant girlfriend, Dani, and her two other guys, including Mr. Armstrong. I quickly look away. He's already warned me about my part in tonight's event and I can't get nervous or I might fuck it up.

I also note Alexsei Ryan and Coach Phillips sitting together with the amazingly gorgeous Luna, and her other guy, the dude who sits with her at games now.

I hate that guy.

In the next section over I note Luna and Dani's friend Elise with Justin Travers. I pull up a little straighter because she's hot and I think single. Except I'm not the only one who's noticed. Travers is totally flirting with the curvy brunette.

And as I glance at our net, I notice that Wilder is watching Travers and Elise with narrowed eyes.

I don't know what the hell that means other than no pussy for Wade yet again with all these damn hockey players around.

The crowd representing the charity the dragon is playing for—a multi-state literacy program—goes crazy.

The Dallas dragon has shot the puck directly past Blake Wilder and the kid he's supposed to be coaching.

Not only is there no love for Wade, that fucking dragon just beat me because Wilder was distracted.

I blow out a breath. Dammit. These women are becoming a real problem for the Racketeers.

I mean, I understand women being a distraction, but these guys have got to play hockey around here. Then again, if any hot girl in her twenties shows me any sort of attention, I will be beyond distracted.

The dragon skates up to me, hip bumps me, then skates off toward the hallway that will lead to the locker rooms.

I start after him. I need to figure out what the hell is going on. Do I know this guy or something? Do I owe him money? Have we smoked weed together before?

Maybe I owe him money for the weed.

I step off the ice and head down the short hallway. I'm needed up in the stands in about two minutes, but I want to find out what this guy's deal is.

"Hey, yo!" I call out, pulling my Malamute head off.

The dragon turns, squares up, then pulls his head off.

Holy shit.

Long blonde hair tumbles out from underneath the green scaly head.

Yeah. I don't owe this guy money for weed.

This is no guy.

And if I'd smoked weed with this girl, I would absolutely remember it.

I'd remember doing anything with this girl.

"Hey, Wade," she says in a sweet, flirty voice.

"Uh. Hey."

"You coming to the get together later?" She rests the dragon head on her hip, draping her arm over the top of it.

I have no idea what she looks like underneath the rest of that green and gold costume, and I don't care. Those eyes, that hair, those lips…I'm in.

"Absolutely."

"Great. I'll see you there."

I watch her walk away and realize that fuck, I'm gonna need to get on that group chat after all because I have no idea what get together she's talking about and I now need to.

I'm tempted to go after her, but then I hear Crew McNeill's voice boom out over the PA system. "Hey everybody! Thanks for coming out to Feeling Pucky!"

The crowd cheers.

"And if you'll hang out for just one more minute, I have something else I'd like you to see."

That's my cue.

I shoot one last parting glance down the hallway at the dragon, who has just turned the corner. Then I put my head back on and start for the stands.

CHAPTER 18
Dani

"WHAT'S HE DOING?" I ask Michael.

Michael just gives me a wink and a smile. "Just being Crew."

That means he knows, but he's not telling.

I look back to center ice. Yeah, this is Crew. This could be almost anything.

I sit back in my seat, rest my hands on my belly and grin, waiting to see what my boyfriend is up to. Other than being Chicago's favorite hockey player, of course.

I feel warmth spread through my chest. Crew is in his element. He loves the spotlight. Loves making the fans grin and cheer. Loves this arena.

A year ago I would have said this was home to him. Now I know it's his second home. Our house, our family—me, Michael, and Nathan—is his first home.

I'm so happy to see him down on the ice, grinning, and being his charming self with the crowd. I think he's truly over the championship loss. I'm sure he still has regrets if he thinks about it, but he's moved on. The whole team has. The event tonight was fun. Everybody turned out and interacted with the fans, cheered for their charities, and had a great time egging on the mascots and their goalies. The most important part is that the kids had a great time and they raised a ton of money.

And that Crew knows this is where he belongs. Chicago. With the Racketeers.

With us.

"As you all know, my life has been pretty exciting this past year," Crew says.

The crowd cheers and I smile, looking around.

I never would've expected the incredibly warm welcome and acceptance our foursome would get from the city of Chicago and all of the Racketeers fans. There are still a few haters here and there, but every time there is a negative comment posted anywhere online, at least twenty people jump on to defend us and say how great they think everything is.

I look over at Luna and she gives me a wink.

It doesn't hurt that Alexsei Ryan is also wildly popular and is also in a foursome relationship that includes Crew McNeill's sister.

They are both beloved by the Racketeers fandom and they've just given everyone even more reason to understand and support nontraditional relationships.

"And most of you know, my family is expecting even more excitement here in a few months." Crew pauses again as there are more cheers. "In case you're not caught up," he says. "Cookie and Company is expanding. We're having a baby just before Christmas."

Louder cheers erupt and both Nathan and Michael reach over at the same time and squeeze my knees.

"I know most of you also know that my beautiful, amazing girlfriend got married a few months ago. To my two best friends," Crew says with a chuckle. "And I am so happy. They are amazing. I can't imagine having our lives in any other way."

I feel my eyes stinging. It's obvious he's happy. No one watching him or listening could doubt that for a second.

"Well," he says. "Maybe there is *one* thing I could imagine another way."

I sit up as Crew's eyes land on me. He smiles.

"Dani," Luna says.

I ignore her.

There's something in Crew's eyes that I can't look away from.

"*Dani*," Luna says again.

"Not now," I mutter.

"Danielle," Nathan says.

I frown. I'm still watching Crew. He's not saying anything. He just lifts his hand and points at me.

"*Danielle*," Nathan repeats.

I finally look at him. "What?"

He points. I follow his finger to the end of our row. Standing in the aisle is Sammy the Malamute.

He motions with his hand that I am supposed to come to him.

I laugh and shake my head.

He nods and then points. I look up to see us up on the KissCam.

Of course we are.

I'm actually surprised that Nathan hasn't removed that thing. He keeps threatening to.

I shake my head and point at Crew. "I need to stay here," I tell Sammy.

He motions again, and I shake my head.

The crowd is cheering and starts chanting, "Sammy! Sammy! Sammy!"

Michael leans over and says, "Go with him."

I look at him in surprise. "What?"

Michael lifts my hand to his lips and presses a kiss to my knuckles. "Go."

Suddenly, my heart is pounding.

I look at Nathan.

He gives me a smile, then leans in and kisses my temple. "Go," he says too.

I swallow hard.

Then I look at Sammy.

He gives me another "come here" motion and I feel Nathan and Michael helping me to my feet. They pass me over to Sammy, who I expect to take my hand. Instead, he leans over and scoops me up into his arms.

I gasp.

The crowd is now going wild.

I look back to the ice.

To Crew.

He has his hands tucked in his pockets and he's watching me with a huge smile. He's so handsome. So happy. So...

Mine.

He's mine.

I can see it in his eyes. I can *feel* it, even with several yards between us.

And I suddenly know what's about to happen.

Right here, where it all began.

I give him a grin even as my eyes fill with tears. Then I loop my arm around Sammy's furry neck and let him carry me down to the ice.

He skates me out to the center of the Racketeers' rink, and sets me on my feet in front of Crew.

But before he lets me go, he dips me back and plants a kiss right on my mouth.

Well, kind of. He puts his fake-fur covered mascot mouth over mine, covering most of my face.

I start laughing as the arena goes crazy and Crew says, "Hey, that wasn't part of the script."

Sammy straightens and makes sure I'm steady on my feet before he lets go. Then he says, "I'm feeling lucky tonight."

Crew just shakes his head.

I watch as Sammy looks in Nathan's direction and gives him a wave.

My husband is scowling at him.

"God, Mr. Armstrong is scary as fuck," he says, shaking his head.

I laugh as he skates off.

"Dani girl."

I turn to face Crew. "Hey."

"You know what's going on, right?"

"I think so."

"If you don't want me to do this like this, I'll make up something else for the crowd," he tells me, his words just for us. "I'll make it quiet and sweet and just us. But," he says, stepping close and lifting a hand to cup my cheek. "Big and loud and awesome and for everyone to see is how I intend to love you for the rest of my life."

I suck in a little breath and my heart squeezes so hard in my chest I think it stops for nearly three seconds.

He drags his thumb over my cheek and I realize I'm crying.

"So, I have a very strong urge to do this big and loud and awesome and for everyone to see."

I press my lips together.

This is Crew. The third man I've chosen to love, to make a life with. This is how he lives and loves and how I love being loved by him.

I grasp his wrist and squeeze. "This is what you bring to my life, Crew. The big and loud and awesome that I need. That I want."

His smile is huge and bright. "I love you so damned much."

"I love you too."

Suddenly, he drops to one knee and puts the microphone to his mouth. "Danielle, you are the first, and only thing in my life, that has ever been more important, and more fun, than hockey."

There is laughter, and cheering around us, but I can't look away from Crew's beloved face.

"Don't tell the fans, but if I had to choose between you and hockey, I'd choose you every time."

I laugh at the adorable grin he's giving me. The grin I know I will still be seeing on this man's face even when he's eighty years old. He's going to be the mischief, the spontaneity, and the cause of belly laughs in my life until the day I die.

The fans are mostly laughing, though there are a few boos peppered in now.

That just makes Crew and I both laugh harder.

He sobers slightly and looks me directly in the eyes. "Dani, you're not getting rid of me. I'm in this for the long haul. For all the couch buying, all the movie nights, all the family holidays, all the quiet times, all the craziness, all the babies—" His voice wobbles a little on that word and I run my fingers through his hair. "All the hockey wins and losses…" He clears his throat. "All of life's wins and losses."

I lift my own hand to wipe my tears this time.

"Let's get married," he says. "Let's make it official. Wear my ring…too." He grins as he glances in Nathan and Michael's direction. Then he looks back at me. "Be my wife."

I'm nodding before he even finishes. "Yes. Definitely yes."

His eyes are shining with love and happiness. He lifts the microphone to my mouth. "One more time for the fans, sweet girl."

I laugh, but lean in and say clearly and loudly through the PA system of the Racketeers arena. "I love you so much. Yes, I'll marry you, Crew McNeill."

CHAPTER 19
Crew

NATHAN AND MICHAEL meet us as I carry Dani off the ice.

I give her another long, lingering kiss, and then pass her over to her husbands.

They both kiss her, but I also get one armed hugs and a, "I'm so happy for you," from Michael, and a, "You did good," from Nathan.

I am so fucking happy.

I can't believe that I put this off for this long.

Still, I have to admit that proposing to my girl on this ice in front of this crowd was perfect.

I know we're going to be all over social media, if we're not already, and the sports page, as well as probably some of the sports talk shows, will be talking about this.

Dani and our family are more important than hockey, but I sure don't mind when it all mixes together.

Everything started in this arena, actually right by these seats. This is essentially where I came up off the ice and first kissed Dani when I saw her up on the KissCam.

The rightness of all of this moment hits me directly in the chest.

I watch as my sister enfolds Dani in a huge hug, tears in her eyes, and says something to her that I can't hear. I've watched these two together for so many years that it just seems obvious they will be in each other's life forever. But now I've made it officially official.

Elise, Cam, and even Sammy all hug Dani.

And now I need some alone time.

Or at least time with Dani and the guys.

I grab her by the hips and pull her back against me. "Time to head home," I say in her ear.

She's been mine for months, but there is definitely something about knowing she's going to be my *wife* that makes my possessiveness feel even stronger.

If this is what Nathan and Michael have been feeling for the past several weeks, I'm not surprised that, more than ever, there's rarely a time one of them isn't touching her, holding her, hugging her.

I need her. That's often true but suddenly I *need* her. *Right now*.

"No way, we're going out to celebrate," my sister tells me, a hand on her hip.

I shake my head. "Another time."

"You pulled your head out of your ass and proposed to my best friend. Dani is now going to be my *sister*." Luna actually looks a little choked up. "We are *celebrating*."

Dani laces her fingers with mine and looks up. "Maybe for a little bit?" she says.

I give her a look, then lean down and say in her ear, "I've never had fiancée pussy before, and I need it right *now*. Find a way to make that happen and we can go anywhere you want to after."

Her fingers tighten on mine, and she says to Luna, "We can meet you at the bar."

My sister's grin is bright. "Great." She looks around.

I know the moment her gaze lands on Alexsei. Her whole face softens and I can literally see how in love she is. *Wow*.

"As soon as I round up my men, we'll head over there and get a table." She looks at Elise. "You coming?"

Elise is looking at something over Luna's shoulder. I turn to look and if I didn't know better, I'd think she was watching Wilder and Hayes.

"Is the whole team coming?" Elise asks.

Luna shrugs. "We can invite them. They're almost always up for a party. And this is a pretty good reason."

Elise flips her hair over her shoulder. "Maybe. I might have plans." She glances in the other direction, where the Dragons' players are gathered, chatting.

Luna laughs. "Or you could have plans and then *more* plans after that."

Elise laughs. "Maybe."

I don't know what's going on. I only know what my plans are. I squeeze Dani's hips. "Let's go."

Nathan pulls his phone out of his pocket. "I'll text Andrew."

Dani reaches out and touches his arm. "Not yet."

He looks at her questioningly. "Why?"

She looks up at me with a flirtatious smile. "I need to go up to your office."

"You left something in my office?" Nathan asks, clearly confused.

She lifts a shoulder. "Let's just say there's something in your office that I need."

I catch on immediately. I love this girl. She is always up to play with me. Us. And that makes me as hard as anything.

"Great idea." I take her hand and start up the steps, my focus on the elevator that will take us to Nathan's office upstairs. No one will be up there, no one will bother us, and we can do whatever the fuck we want.

"Come on," Dani says, motioning for both Nathan and Michael to come with us.

As if they wouldn't have followed. I am taking their sexy, sweet wife up to Nathan's office. There's no way they were letting us go alone.

And I'm guessing it's only taking them about two seconds to catch on to what's going to happen when we get there.

None of us talk as we walk down the deserted hallway to the elevator and get on but as soon as the elevator doors slide shut, Nathan asks, "You can't even wait 'til you get home, naughty girl?"

She smiles. "I just got engaged to a very hot, charming, talented hockey player. I am very horny right now."

Nathan just watches her with a hot gaze, but Michael gives a low groan.

"Besides," Dani says, looking at each of us. "That office is where we started."

That's true. The very first night we all met her, the four of us ended up in Nathan's office. And not long after, Nathan called Michael and I in to stake his claim. It was then that we first proposed the idea of sharing her.

I turn and crowd her against the elevator wall. "You know that all three of us wanted you that night, right? That you could have snapped your fingers and taken any of us home with you?" I ask, lifting my hand and running my fingers through her hair.

She pulls her lower lip between her teeth and nods. Then her gaze flickers to something—or someone—over my shoulder. "I *did* take Michael home with me," she says with a sexy little smile.

"You sure did," he says.

I run my hand up her thigh. "That's right. You've been needy and greedy from the very beginning, haven't you?" She's wearing a one-piece jumpsuit that makes it easy to run my hand up to her ass and squeeze.

"I have been for you three," she says.

"And we should have just stripped you down and taken you all together that very first night in Boss's office," I say, dropping my face to her neck and dragging my mouth from her collarbone to her ear. "You would have let us. You would have happily spread these pretty legs, bent over that desk, and let us have this perfect pussy even that first night, wouldn't you?"

She lets her head drop back against the wall of the elevator. "Probably," she admits.

"Probably?" I bite down on her neck. "You were ours from minute one, Dani."

She moans and arches closer to me. "I was."

The elevator arrives on the top floor just then and the doors swish open. I bend and pick Dani up in one smooth motion. She gasps but grins up at me. "I can walk."

"Not fast enough." I stride out of the elevator and down the short hall to Nathan's office.

The other two are right behind us. I haven't choreographed this encounter, but it will be fun. And it *is* Nathan's office so I suppose he can have some say. I don't want to break any lamps or anything.

I stop by the door and wait for Nathan to unlock it. Then I step through and look around. He does have a couch in here. It's leather and doesn't look that comfortable, but it would totally work. There's also the desk and the two chairs that are always in front, facing his huge high-backed I'm-the-CEO leather chair behind the desk.

"Clear anything off your desk you don't want getting wrinkled or…" I look down at Dani and give her a wink. "…wet."

Her cheeks get pink, which cracks me up even as it makes me love her even more. After all of the many deliciously dirty things the *three* of us have done to this girl, I can still make her blush.

Jesus, she's adorable.

Nathan doesn't argue, which is surprising and awesome. He just moves to the desk and begins clearing things off the top. It's lucky that he's a pretty neat guy. There's not a lot there. He slides a few things into his desk drawers. There's so little there I wonder what the hell he actually does in this office.

I walk Dani over to the desk and perch her on the edge of it, facing the boss's chair. She automatically shifts her knees apart in obvious invitation. Damn, our girl likes to get fucked. I step in between her legs and take her mouth with mine for a brief, hard kiss.

The hitch in her breath has me instantly hard.

"Do me a favor, Doc, and free these pretty little tits for me," I say as I brush my fingers over her nipples.

The jumpsuit doesn't have a zipper, it just slips off of her shoulders, so when Michael steps in behind her, he's able to ease the fabric down until it's puddled around her waist. "Or not-so-little tits," I murmur, in awe at how the pregnancy is changing Dani's body. Her breasts are full, spilling out of her bra in a tempting display I can't fucking resist.

I bend down and suck the swell of flesh. Her hands come to rest on my shoulders. Nathan has come around the desk to perch in his ridiculously big chair, hands on his knees, leaning forward to take in the view. Michael undoes Dani's bra, easing his hands around her back to cup her tits.

Dani gives a soft moan. God, she's even more sensitive now with all the hormones than ever before. I take her nipple into my mouth and tug the bud before giving a light nip. Her response is immediate and gratifying. Her fingers dig into my shoulders, her head tilts back, her back arching to press herself more fully into my mouth.

"Crew, please. I need more."

"Oh, I know you do. Trust me, pretty girl, you'll get more." I cup her pussy, massaging her clit over the soft fabric of her jumpsuit. "You're going to spread your legs for all three of us. It's a special day so we're all going to take turns with this sweet little pussy."

Dani nods eagerly.

Michael takes the initiative to ease her back down onto the desk. I grip her behind the knees and shift her closer to the edge so her legs dangle over. Michael goes and plucks a decorative pillow off of the couch and shifts it under Dani's head while I tug her clothes off fully and toss the one-piece outfit back onto Nathan's lap.

He gives me a brief look before lifting the fabric to his nose and breathing in deeply.

Damn.

I turn my attention back to Dani and that little scrap of lace that is standing between me and her pussy. Running my finger down the front of her panties, I press in, so that the lace sinks into her slit. She whimpers. The fabric comes back damp.

"Wet already," I tell the other guys. "I'm going first then you can fight each other to be second." I lift my finger to my mouth and suck on it. I can faintly taste her essence.

"Doc, you take her second," Nathan says.

Which sounds generous, but if I know the boss, it's all part of his plan to be able to fuck her immediately after she comes on his tongue. Nathan prefers her pussy over getting sucked or taking her ass. Whereas I like any and everything Dani will let me do to her equally.

Also, Nathan's crazy if he thinks he's getting in our girl first when she just said yes to my marriage proposal.

Dani is staring up at me, wide-eyed, her chest rising up and down rapidly as she fights for control. I know our girl and she wants to lift her hips, urge me onto her. Even as the thought floats through my head, she does exactly that, lifting and wiggling.

"*Crew.*"

"Shh," I tell her. "I just want to tease you a little." I drop between her legs and ease her panties down her thighs, nuzzling my lips along her soft skin.

Dani is already trembling with need. I glance up and see that Michael is working her nipples between his thumbs and forefingers, while she turns her head toward him, seeking more. She wants his cock in her mouth but I think the angle is off.

"Be patient," I add.

She's really rocking her hips now, trying to entice me. "Crew, *please.*"

"Please, what?" I lightly draw my finger up her inner thigh and rest it at her pussy, just letting it hover there.

"Do something. I need you. We're *engaged* now."

I groan. She knows me so fucking well. She knows that little reminder is all it takes to make me hard as steel. Still, I'm in charge here and this woman is mine and I'm going to drive her out of her mind with need before I show her that I will always give her *exactly* what she wants and needs. Every damned time.

"What do you think you want?" I ease just the tip of my finger into her pussy.

"Fuck me."

"Oh, you don't want my tongue on this sweet little cunt?"

"Yes," she moans.

"Do you want me to fuck you or to eat you? Tell me, sweetheart." My own need has my mouth hot and my dick throbbing, but I could do this all day—tease her into oblivion. I love being surrounded by her thighs, breathing in the scent of her arousal, knowing that in this moment I could ask her to do anything and she would.

She's so fucking sexy.

"Both!" Dani sobs.

That makes me smile against her flesh.

"Poor girl. You don't even know. You just need to trust me to give you everything you need *when* you need it." I give her the full length of my finger as I slide my tongue over her clit, swirling around the taut button. Dani gives a cry of pleasure and approval. I add a second finger, matching the rhythm of my fingers and my tongue and almost immediately I sense she's going to come.

I pull away entirely, breathing hard, ripping my shirt off as I gesture to Nathan.

Dani gives a sob of disappointment. "Don't stop. Oh my God, I can't…"

"Get in there," I tell Nathan. "You're closer."

Nathan doesn't really like to be told what to do when we're worshiping Dani, but he readily complies, burying his mouth between her thighs and lapping at her pussy.

I take the opportunity to ditch my shoes and strip off my

pants. Michael undoes his shirt and peels it off.

"Should we let her come?" Michael asks me, his voice thick with desire. He has his hand on his cock, stroking it over his pants.

Even though Dani has multiple orgasms on a regular basis, I love watching her go wild from want. "Not a chance."

Nathan obviously agrees. He pulls away, wiping his mouth, eyes dark even as Dani tries to reach for him, half-sitting up. He stands up and strips his suit jacket off. "Let's hold her down, McNeill."

Dani is panting and sneaks her hand between her legs to try to stroke herself.

"Now that is a very naughty girl," I tell her, gripping her hand and lifting it away right before she can touch herself. "There will be punishment for that. But first, Michael gets a little taste."

Michael shifts around the desk and Armstrong and I each take one of Dani's hands and ease her back down onto the desk. Her eyes are glassy, cheeks pink, nipples tight. Goosebumps trail down her arms. Michael buries his tongue in her but she's too close to coming so he's barely there before he lifts his mouth. Then he descends on her again, tongue flicking over her clit before he pulls back. He does it over and over, giving her only the briefest contact each time and she's shaking and sobbing.

"Michael," she begs. "*More*."

"What do you think needs to happen now, Dani girl?" I ask her, easing my finger between her lips.

She sucks it greedily, which makes me swear under my breath.

"You fuck me?" she asks around my now-wet finger.

"Try again," I tell her.

"I should be punished?"

"Exactly."

"Good girl," Nathan says, lifting her arm and kissing the inside of her forearm. "Good girls know they need to be punished when they've been naughty."

Dani nods eagerly. "Yes...Daddy."

All three of us suck in quick, audible breaths.

"*Fuck*, Dani," I groan, grabbing my dick and adjusting myself.

Nathan looks feral. She's never called him, or anyone, Daddy before and he clearly fucking loves it.

Michael, who is usually the slow, gentle one, is having the same reaction. "Let her hands go," he demands, with a hard, clipped tone.

We do and he helps her up off of the desk. He gives her a hard kiss, his fingers sawing in and out of her pussy while he does, before quickly spinning her around to face the chair. "Hold on to the arms."

Dani does, leaning forward and gripping the two arms of Nathan's desk chair, her tight ass rising for us to spank.

I want to smack her, but I'd rather look into her eyes while Nathan is doing it. So I say, "Let me in here," and lightly tap her arm.

She raises it and I take a seat in Nathan's chair, so when her palm lands on the arm again, we're inches apart, eyes locked on each other. She's breathing hard, her tongue slipping over her bottom lip.

"This is a great chair," I say, settling back, legs spread out. "Very comfortable, Boss."

Nathan is behind Dani now, running his hands over her bare ass. "Only the best," he says, conversationally.

"Is this leather?" I say, gaze still on Dani. "I need a new gaming chair."

Her jaw drops, like she can't believe we're being so casual. She looks ready to protest when Nathan gives her ass a smack. She jerks a little, making her tits bounce and her eyes drift shut.

"It probably doesn't have the neck support you need," Nathan says, as if he didn't just spank our girl.

"Gaming chairs are much more ergonomic," Michael adds, coming to Dani's side and cupping her breast, teasing the nipple.

Nathan smacks Dani's ass again and Michael pinches her nipple.

She bites her lip to prevent a moan escaping. She has decided to play the game with us. She doesn't protest.

"That is true." I pull my dick out of my pants and give it a few hard pumps as Nathan settles into a rhythm of his palm connecting with Dani's ass. "But I like the bounce this one has."

The crack of Nathan's palm has me fighting for control. Dani's eyes fly open and there's desperation in them. I watch as her husbands work her over right in front of me. God she's gorgeous, taking whatever we give her, playing whatever games we concoct. She trusts us so implicitly it makes my chest ache. And makes me want to give her the whole fucking world.

"I wonder how much weight it holds," Michael remarks, playing with her tits.

"Enough for this girl to climb on Crew and ride his cock," Nathan says.

Her sweet little ass must be turning pink by now. Nathan moves his hand lower and taps her pussy from behind.

Then she shocks all of us, herself included, by giving a low moan in the back of her throat and spasming against his palm. Her eyes slide shut and her head drops forward and her shoulders tense.

She's coming.

Just from being spanked.

I lose the thread of our ridiculous conversation as I watch in awe as she rides out the wave of a tight orgasm.

The other guys seem equally as astonished and turned on. Nathan turns her again.

"On Crew's cock," he orders. "Now."

Dani doesn't need any other encouragement. Her hair hits me in the face as she seats herself down on my dick in one eager push and suddenly I'm surrounded by her slick heat.

Groaning, I grip her hips as I help her pump up and down on me.

Michael holds her hair back so he can watch as Nathan eases his own cock between her lips and we find a rhythm together.

CHAPTER 20
Nathan

WE'RE all happy that Crew finally proposed to Danielle. As she bobs her head over my dick repeatedly, the smooth silken heat of her tongue setting my nerve endings aflame, I'm even more thrilled.

Danielle is in a good mood and feeling loved means we're all getting the benefit of her *very* eager affection.

God, I love this woman and how unapologetically sexual she is.

I'm also constantly so fucking grateful that no other man turned the key on unlocking this sexual goddess before we came along.

She's ours and we are the only ones who can properly worship her.

Michael takes her hands then and moves them behind her back, holding her wrists together with one big hand. The position causes her back to arch and her to fully trust us to hold her up and control her body.

That fills me with love and desire in equal measure. She will let us do anything to her. She'll fully give herself to us over and over again. Not just physically, though certainly that, but her heart, her life, her time and energy, her soul.

Seeing her seated on Crew, fully naked, giving soft moans of approval around my cock as he thrusts up into her is so damn hot. She loves being tied up, spanked, teased and praised. She's submissive and enthusiastic and can never get enough of us.

And now she called me *daddy*. I nearly lost control right then and there.

That is definitely going to keep happening.

"This chair is fucking amazing," Crew says. His hands grip her hips tighter, making red marks on her pale skin. "Almost as amazing as your goddamned perfect pussy, baby. *Damn*."

Danielle nods in approval, never releasing her hold on me. I gather her hair in one hand, holding it back so I can watch her pink lips sliding over me, causing my balls to tighten.

"This is the one and only time you sit in this chair, McNeill."

His head is back now and he doesn't bother to respond. I can see he's too lost in fucking Danielle now. It makes me thrust deeper between Danielle's lips.

"That's it," Michael encourages. "You good, pretty girl? Spread your legs further if your belly is in the way."

That's Hughes. Always our voice of reason.

Danielle pulls back off of me long enough to reassure Michael. "It feels *so good*."

I hiss and push her back onto me. I can't get enough of her.

Michael's taken the time to strip his clothes off and he's squeezing his erection, watching the action with hooded eyes.

Crew smacks the side of her ass. "Come for me, sweet thing. I can't hold out. You feel too tight and wet for me to last any longer."

We're all losing control.

None more than Danielle. She's desperately trying to help Crew now, bouncing up and down on him, her jaw going slack as she lets me thrust in and out of her mouth. Her eyes are watering from my dick deep in her throat.

"That's it, naughty girl," Michael tells her. "Come all over Crew, baby. Give your fiancé all your sweetness."

Her whole body is trembling, her skin stained pink from exertion and arousal. My hands are fisted in her hair and as much as I love the moments I have alone with Danielle, this is where I'm continually in awe with her—having all three of us loving and worshiping her completes her. Which completes me.

Danielle's eyes screw tightly shut and she convulses. I know she's coming from her expression and from Crew's reaction.

"Holy *fuck*. You're working me so damn good." He lets out a groan. "Yes, baby. Fucking yes."

There's no point in holding back myself. "Open your throat, dirty girl, I'm done." I release into her warm mouth in thick pulsating ropes of pleasure.

She opens her eyes even as the last vestiges of her orgasm shudder through her and we lock gazes as she sucks in every last drop of my essence, swallowing with my cock still resting on her lips. She flicks her tongue over the tip, like she hasn't had enough.

Un-fucking-believable. That's what she is.

I step back, letting out the breath I've been holding.

Michael and I exchange a look. I give him a nod.

His turn.

The silent language we've learned over the last year allows us to all enjoy Danielle together and give her what she needs. I need a minute to regroup, but our girl will not be satisfied yet.

Michael helps her off the chair, wrapping his arms around her to steady her. "You need me to fill you up some more, pretty girl?"

"Yes." Her head bobs eagerly.

"Here, lay on your forearms on the desk so you're far enough back from the edge to make room for your belly." He uses his large hands to guide her, his touch obviously gentle.

Crew looks wrecked but the minute Danielle bends over according to Michael's instructions he sits up straighter before resting his forearms on his thighs so he can get closer to watch. Danielle's tight ass lifting again in the air has my mouth hot. My cock stirs again. Smacking her ass is something I never get tired of and I greedily reach out and run my palm over her lightly before shifting fully out of the way.

Michael moves in behind her and when he takes her, she gasps. His thrusts are powerful, rapid, and I know exactly how he's feeling—like he never wants to be anywhere but in that pussy.

"Give that little pussy what it needs," I encourage, running a hand over my cock so I can be ready again for her.

Crew is doing the same.

We should let Michael get her off and explode himself, then head home before continuing, but we're all raw and emotional and turned on by our girl, so I'm not sure that's going to happen. We might be here all damn night.

Michael runs one big hand up and down her back as he fucks her. "Press back, sweet girl," he murmurs. "That's it. Take me deep."

"Oh, my God, Michael," Dani says breathlessly. "You're so big and I'm so sensitive."

"You feel like fucking heaven," he tells her, sliding his hand around to first cup her belly, then lower to play with her clit. "So hot. So wet. So damned perfect."

She reaches back and grasps his hip, clutching him closer. "It's all so good. It's almost too much."

Doc picks up the pace, fucking her faster. "You can take it. It's never too much for this perfect, greedy little pussy."

"Oh, God," she moans.

"You're going to come again," I tell her, moving closer. I lean over and clasp her chin, looking directly into her eyes. "And then again. You're not going to be able to walk out of here, Danielle. You're going to have our cum filling you up and running down your leg as we *carry* you out of here."

She moans and Michael gives a low, "*Fuck*. She likes that."

I run my fingers through her hair. "Our perfect, sweet, amazing girl. You have no idea how much we love that you're also our perfect dirty slut."

"*Yes,*" Michael says through gritted teeth, clearly responding to Danielle's pussy's response. "Grip me like that, Dani. Milk me."

I love that this sweet woman loves dirty talk. I doubt anyone who has met her in her quaint little bookshop, or watched her cheering for Crew in her Racketeers gear, or seen her smiling sweetly and walking between the three of us as we go out to dinner, as if she's this meek little thing that needs her big men protecting her, would believe how she loves our filthy words and, even more, our filthy actions.

I reach underneath her and pluck at a nipple as I lean in to kiss her. I stroke my tongue along hers deeply, then say, "You need to come around your husband's cock, my beautiful dirty girl, so your other husband can fuck you and then your fiancé can make you come *again*."

Of course, that's what does it. Our girl comes hard, with a loud cry, gripping my hand, and Michael's hip as she shatters.

Nearly a half hour later, Danielle is limp and spent. Crew gathers her up into his arms and carries her to the couch. He's peppering her with sweet, devotional kisses.

"I'm going to have to redecorate," I say as I zip my pants back up. "I will never be able to look at this desk or chair again without getting hard."

Danielle gives a soft giggle, her arms around Crew's neck. "I would hate to distract you from work."

"Liar," I chuckle.

"Do you really believe he works in here?" Crew asks, shooting me a grin. "I mean, seriously, what *do* you do?"

I roll my eyes.

"Careful, McNeill," Michael says. "He is still your boss. Which means we might have crossed a line or two here."

That makes me laugh. "I think we did that a long time ago. But we said no work at home. Guess we forgot to say no sex at work."

"I'm not complaining," Crew says. "Dani, you complaining?"

She shakes her head. "I'm having a major boss/secretary fantasy right now."

That makes me groan. "*Damn.* Let's get you home and we can discuss your duties and salary in further detail."

Michael lifts Danielle's jumpsuit off of the floor and carries it over to her. "I think she should have to interview for the position. *Really* convince you that she wants this job. That she'll do *anything* to work for you."

My wife's eyes widen. "Oh, yes, of course. Mr. Armstrong. I'm highly qualified for the position and I excel at attention to detail. I'll be very...dutiful."

That's all it takes. I point to the door. "Home. Now. Before I spank you again."

"That's an empty threat," Crew points out. "I'm ordering food to be delivered here. We're not getting home for hours because I *have* to see Dani's job interview. And this swanky-ass office is perfect for this."

I look to Hughes. "Thoughts? Help?"

He shrugs and chuckles. "That does sound really fucking hot."

Danielle stands up and walks slowly toward me, confident in her naked body and the hold she has over me. Her fingers trail down over her nipples. "Would you like to hear about my experience?"

"Yes."

She takes a seat in the chair on the opposite side of the desk from mine. She crosses her legs tightly, straightens her back and rests her hands on her lap on top of her pussy.

"Order takeout in," I bark to Crew. "We have a lot of work to do. We might be pulling an all-nighter."

CHAPTER 21
Nathan

"OF COURSE he turned this into a circus." I'm grinning, though, as Michael and I climb the stairs to our bedroom.

Michael laughs. "Well, it's actually more of a carnival."

I am as surprised as anyone that I'm enjoying this.

Danielle and Crew are having their commitment ceremony at our house. Okay, technically *outside* our house. Crew was even responsible enough to get the permits needed. And there were a few. Not just to shut down the street in front of the house for the food trucks, but also to make room for the Ferris wheel, carnival games, and the two hot air balloons.

When I say he's turning it into a circus, I mean it.

The only thing he didn't do was bring in live animals, or clowns.

He mentioned animals and thank God, Danielle and Michael both talked him out of that.

Yes, all of the neighborhood kids would have loved pony rides and a petting zoo, but that was over the top, especially for an event that is supposed to be a wedding, not a county fair.

Thank God clowns didn't even occur to him. Or at least he didn't say them out loud to me.

As much as I love our baby-on-the-way and any future children we're going to have, the three other parents are going to have to handle any and all clown duty.

Michael and I stop outside of the bedroom door. He looks at me. "Are you ready to walk our wife down the aisle?"

I chuckle. "None of this is ever going to not sound strange is it?"

He shakes his head with a grin. "Probably not. But then again, it's very us."

I'm in a great mood. Probably because Danielle has been glowing even more brightly ever since Crew proposed a week ago. The only reason they've waited even a week to have the ceremony is because of the huge production Crew is making it into.

But they deserve to do whatever they want to do with this day. Had I given it any thought at all, I would've realized there was no way Crew McNeill was going to have an understated ceremony like the one Michael and I had with Danielle.

The guy thinks the NCAA Final Four deserves a party even when he doesn't care about any of the teams playing. Of course he's going to think his *wedding* needs to be a blow-out.

This production outside is perfect for them. Crew is the sunshine, the laughter, the silly, and the spontaneity in Danielle's life. And Michael and I are not just fine with that, we're happy about it.

In the end, it worked out great that they are having their ceremony separate from ours, so that they can have it exactly the way they want it.

Most of our commitment ceremony with our girl was my influence. I had always pictured it sophisticated, but simple. Michael, on the other hand, didn't care about specific details. He just wanted Danielle walking down that aisle toward him and saying 'I do'.

Michael lifts his hand and knocks on the door.

"Come in," Danielle calls softly.

Michael opens the door and pushes it open, letting me step in first.

It's rare for a man to see his wife on her wedding day to another man.

But emotion hits me the moment my eyes land on her.

She's not dressed in white. Instead, because the ceremony is outside and it is August in Chicago, she's dressed in a multi-colored, spaghetti-strapped sundress that falls to her ankles. It's fitted against her breasts, but then flares out over the slight swell of her belly. Her hair is up, twisted into a pretty updo that also keeps her neck bare and cool.

Her makeup is simple, and the only jewelry she's wearing are the two bands that Michael and I placed on her finger a few months ago.

She looks absolutely gorgeous.

She is everything I have ever wanted and, strangely, I cannot wait to take her downstairs and watch her marry Crew.

"You're radiant," Michael tells her, crossing the room. He takes her hands and leans over to press a kiss against her cheek.

She looks up at him with a sweet smile. "Thank you. I'm so excited."

"Not nervous at all?" I ask as I cross the room to them.

I lean in and kiss her other cheek. I don't want to mess up her lipstick.

"Not nervous. This is going to be so fun." She glances toward the window. "I've been watching them set up."

"You're supposed to be getting ready for your wedding," Michael teases her.

She looks down. "I am ready." Her expression softens. "I've *been* ready for this for a long time."

"I'm glad he finally figured it out," I tell her.

She looks from me to Michael and then back. "Thank you for giving him time. I know it was driving you crazy."

Again, it strikes me how strange it sounds that we would be frustrated about how long it took another man to decide to marry our wife. But I knew this was what Danielle wanted. I also knew it was what Crew wanted deep down. And what we all needed.

"Even though we're a team, we're all still individual people," Michael says. "We all get to figure things out in our own time, in our own way. But we're all going to be there for each other."

"I know," Danielle says, taking Michael's hand in one of hers and grasping mine with her other. "I am so very happy as your wife. If Crew had never come around, I would have felt happy and fulfilled forever. I love you both so much."

I squeeze her hand. "We know that. But we also know that Crew is a part of this, and without him it wouldn't have ever felt complete."

She nods. "Thank you for understanding that."

"Well." I pause, then say, "You're not the only one who loves him."

Her smile is bright. "I love you so much, Nathan Armstrong."

"I love you too. Even though you made me into a soft, mushy, emotional mess."

Michael laughs. "This is a soft, mushy, emotional *mess*?"

I shrug. "Compared to where I started? Yes."

Danielle lifts up on tiptoe and presses a kiss to my cheek. Then she smiles up at Michael. "Just wait until we have a little baby in this house. I think we're going to see a lot of soft and mushy Daddy Nathan."

Michael groans. "You mean *permissive* Daddy Nathan who can't say no to a single pouty lip? I'm afraid you're right."

I laugh. "Is that why I'm excited about the corndogs and winning a stuffed animal at the ring toss? This is my way of nesting?"

Danielle's eyes are sparkling. "Oh, I hope so."

I swat her ass. "Look what you've done to me."

She beams. "By the way, Crew promised me a naughty ride on the Ferris wheel, but I expect both of you to take me on that ride as well."

Michael leans in and captures her lips, clearly not caring about her lipstick. Then he says against her mouth, "Oh, we're going to be taking you on a ride later, Mrs. Armstrong."

A little shiver goes through her and I feel heat tighten my lower body as well. It always does when someone calls her Mrs. Armstrong.

Even if we are minutes away from marrying her off to another man.

Michael straightens and glances at me then he shakes his head. "No."

"What?" I ask.

"Whatever you're thinking. I know that look. Dani has a date with *Crew* downstairs. With our entire family, your hockey team, and our whole neighborhood waiting."

But I look at my wife. "I'll hold that thought till tonight."

She giggles. "But it's my wedding night."

I nod. "Yes, it sure fucking is."

CHAPTER 22
Crew

IT'S ALL ABSOLUTELY PERFECT.

And I don't mean the Ferris wheel, the taco truck, or the hot air balloons that Dani and I are heading for at this very moment.

No, it's the woman next to me and the *reason* we're here.

Dani's hand is tucked in mine. She keeps looking up at me with the sweetest, most loving look on her face, and she fucking smells like cotton candy.

When I met her at the bottom of the stairs, flanked on both sides by Nathan and Michael, I swear I almost cried.

She's so fucking beautiful.

She doesn't look that different today. She wears dresses like this a lot, she wears her hair up like this a lot, her makeup is basic. But today she becomes my wife.

I didn't expect that to feel so different. So big.

But it does.

In this moment I'm glad I waited.

I also know if I said that to Dani, she'd understand.

Things between us haven't technically changed that much since the night Michael proposed. They haven't changed since the night Nathan decided he wanted to propose. They haven't changed that much since the night I explained that I wasn't ready.

I could've proposed that night, and married Dani the same day Nathan and Michael did. Our life wouldn't look different. Our relationship and commitment to one another would be essentially the same.

But this feels better. It feels more serious. I've had time to really think about it. I've seen all of the off-ramps. All of the ways out. I've been reassured by everyone who matters to me that if I didn't do this, I would still be loved, and the rest of my life would still be the same.

I've *chosen* this.

I'm here today with her because we've had the time, gone through the emotions, waded through all of our options.

She's had the chance to see what her life would be like without me.

And it would be pretty damned great, let's be honest.

But she still wants me too.

So *we've* chosen this.

When we make these promises to each other today, we'll both know it's not because we have to, but because we truly *want* to.

"Oh my God, this is so fun," she tells me as I help her up into the hot air balloon.

The guy who's going to be running it for us is the only other person in this basket.

We have two balloons. Both will go several feet up in the air but will stay tethered to the ground. We'll float there for a few minutes, do our vows and everything, and then come back down.

The other basket will hold Michael, Nathan, and our officiant.

They're our witnesses, but they're also the only other people that need to be right in the moment with us.

The rest of the day, however, will be a huge, hilarious, super fun, carnival/over-the-top block party shared with everyone we love.

Our families are here, the entire Racketeers team, including all the behind the scene staff is here, and our whole neighborhood was invited.

By now, they're used to the antics at the Armstrong–Hughes–McNeill house, so everyone turned out, even those who still give us a bit of a side eye.

We figure the kids will be way too busy with the Ferris wheel and the games and the junk food to even ask their parents what this party is all about. No one's going to have to explain how Mrs. Armstrong just got herself another husband.

Once everyone is in the balloons, the operators start lifting us into the air.

I pulled Dani up against my body, nuzzling my face against her neck.

"You used the body spray," I say against her neck. My dick is hardening and I'm going to either throw my new wife over my shoulder and head upstairs for a few minutes after this–which, come to think of it, is a fantastic idea–or I need to keep my hands to myself.

But that's not going to happen.

"Of course," she tells me, running her fingers through my hair. "My husband-to-be gave me a gift this morning. I had to use it."

I'd found the cotton candy scented body spray online and ordered it immediately.

It was the perfect addition to this day.

"It's making me hard, reminding me of all the times we've used that cotton candy, flavored lube," I say against her ear, so the balloon operator can't hear.

She presses against my cock, and I can also feel her pregnant belly press into me. I groan.

"I ordered more of that this week for our wedding night," she tells me.

I lift my head and grin down at her. "Me too."

She laughs. "But I was thinking, we need to grab some real cotton candy to take upstairs tonight." She flutters her eyelashes at me in the playful way that always makes me want to hug her and fuck her at the same time.

I nod. "The minute we get off this balloon I'm grabbing a

couple bags and taking them upstairs to stash so we don't run out," I promise.

She just studies my face, her smile sweet and loving. "I love you so much."

"I have never been happier in my life," I tell her sincerely."Nothing will ever come close to the way you make me feel. Not hockey, not Ferris wheels, not hot air balloons."

"Ditto," she says, sliding her fingers through my hair again. "But hot air balloons and hockey and Ferris wheels *with you*? Perfection."

Soon, we're up as far as we're going to go and the officiant calls from the other basket, "Are you ready?"

I take Dani's hand. "I have never been more ready for anything in my life."

We say our vows, I add my band to the other two on Dani's left hand, I kiss my wife for the first time, and then we grin and wave at the huge crowd of friends and family who are cheering below.

I look over at Nathan and Michael. They're both grinning widely.

Finally, we are *officially*, forever, a family.

CHAPTER 23

Dani

FOUR MONTHS LATER

"I CAN'T BELIEVE it's come to this," I tell Michael as I lounge on our amazing couch. "I'm actually resting a plate on my belly."

The couch is so deep and comfy that I can't really reach the end table and I just absently rested my small plate of cheese and crackers on my stomach.

Michael laughs as he leans over to give me a kiss, straightening his tie. "It makes a convenient shelf, doesn't it?"

"It does." But I decide to set the plate on the couch cushion next to me instead.

I'm huge. I feel huge. I look huge. I'm everything huge. Tits, hips, belly. This baby has taken over my body from head to toe, from my ridiculously shiny hair to my tender nipples, to my decidedly swollen feet, and I'm about as far from comfortable as I've ever been.

Yet, I love it. I *love* being pregnant. I love turning sideways in the mirror and seeing my bump, cupping it in awe with both hands. I love watching my guys stroke their big hands gently over my belly and I love seeing their eyes shine with love for a baby that hasn't even been born yet. Our baby is due in five days and while I've enjoyed my pregnancy, I'm getting very impatient to meet our little guy or girl.

"I'll see you after the game," Michael adds. "McNeill!" he yells up the stairs. "You ready?"

Crew comes running down the stairs, vaulting over the baby gate at the bottom in one smooth action-movie-worthy move that is very sexy.

It's even sexier that he did it while wearing a suit.

He skids to a stop in front of me and bends over to kiss me, and then my belly. "Bye, Dani, bye, Baby. See you at the rink."

"Bye, Crew. Good luck tonight."

"Are you sure you want to come to the game?" Michael says, stepping into his shoes by the front door. "That's a lot of stairs to walk up and down and I know your back hurts."

My back has been my biggest complaint the last two days. It's spasming constantly.

"This house has a lot of stairs," I say, with a grin, glancing over at Nathan as he comes into the living room from the kitchen, carrying two glasses of water. "I think I can handle the arena."

"You're using my own words against me. That hurts." Nathan hands me the water and sets his down on the coffee table.

"It's good for me to keep moving," I tell Michael. "You said that yourself."

"You're right, you're right. I just want to make sure you feel up to it."

"I'm young, I'm healthy, it's important to me to support my husbands and the Racketeers. Besides, once the baby is born, I probably won't step foot out of this house for two weeks. It's going to be January in Chicago and I'm going to be sleep deprived and learning to be a mom. The days are going to fly by. I want to see Luna and Elise tonight."

Nathan is suspiciously looking out the front window. "It looks like it's going to snow. I don't want you going to this game, Danielle."

"Just relax and let her go if she wants," Crew moans. "She's having a baby, not a kidney transplant."

Exactly. "Thank you, Crew." I blow him a kiss.

"She's twenty-five and in great shape. She could pop this baby out tonight and be back at yoga on Monday." Crew grabs his overcoat and slips it on.

That makes me laugh. "Well, that may be overestimating it just a little, sweetheart, but I appreciate your support and confidence in me."

"You can do anything," he says, simply. "I know you can. Have fun hanging out with the girls at the game. Is Cam going to be there?"

I nod. Luna's boyfriend is almost always there with her and tonight is no exception. "I'll see you on the ice."

Michael grabs his coat and kisses me on the top of the head as he heads to the door. "I'll be just a few rows away from you at the game. Text me if you need me."

"Of course. Bye."

Then they leave, a gust of cold wind blowing through the front door on their way out. I shiver and snuggle in next to Nathan, who has settled down on the couch beside me. "It's freezing out there."

"We could just stay home with a roaring fire." He wraps his arm around me and draws me against his chest.

"A gas fireplace doesn't exactly roar."

"But it's cozy here." He squeezes me closer. "The three of you did an amazing job decorating for Christmas."

"For a man who doesn't even like this house, you sure like being in it." Pre-Cookie & Co. Nathan was on the go all the time. Charity events, business meetings, corporate dinners, fundraising benefits—he told me he was almost never in his penthouse before midnight. These days I'm hard-pressed to get him to leave.

I get it. The house is very cozy right now. We have a beautiful live Christmas tree loaded with presents beneath it, garland running down the banister, cinnamon scented candles burning, and a classic wreath on our front door.

"The house has things I would change. But I love the people in it." Nathan runs his palm over my stomach. "I could go two weeks without leaving this house if we're all in it."

"That's probably going to happen sooner than later."

"Which is why we should stay home tonight, in case you go into labor."

I laugh. "No! That's the exact reason we should go out."

"What if you start having contractions?"

"We'll call the doctor. It takes hours before they even want us to go to the hospital. You know that."

He makes a face. "I'll watch *The Holiday* with you if we can stay home."

Now I really laugh. "No, you won't. You'll claim you're going to watch *The Holiday* and by the time Cameron Diaz is dragging her bag up the lane to Kate Winslet's charming country cottage, you'll be trying to have sex."

He makes a face. But he doesn't deny it.

"Remember last Christmas? You had no Christmas tree in your apartment. It looked like the lobby of a hotel in September."

Nathan laughs. "I seem to remember you hanging stockings anyway. What a difference a year makes."

"Yeah," I murmur. "And next year we'll have a one-year-old."

"Exactly. So, we're staying home then," he says. It's not a question. It's a statement.

He's using his bossy Nathan voice. The firm you'll-do-anything-I-say-because-I'm-a-hot-billionaire voice.

"No, we're not. This is what I want and you love me enough to take me to a hockey game, Nathan."

"Shit." He sighs and peels himself off the couch. "Let me take a shower and get dressed. If you have this baby in the hockey arena I am going to be very upset."

"I haven't had any Braxton Hicks in days. I'm not dilated at all. The doctor said I can do all normal activity. And guess what? I know the owner of the Racketeers. I think he can readily get us out of the arena if I do go into labor."

Nathan's expression immediately changes. "Oh, so you know the owner? How, have you fucked him?"

"*So* many times. He has a huge cock." I hold my hand out to him so he can help me off the couch. "Let me take a shower with you."

"I can't ever say no to you."

"You don't have to." I give him a sweet, sassy smile.

"Dani, you look *gorgeous*," Elise says to me as a greeting as I shuffle into the row to take my seat at the Racketeers game.

Nathan is hovering behind me, holding my elbow protectively.

"Aw, thank you. Honestly, aside from the obvious," I say, gesturing to my belly. "I feel pretty good. I've had back pain. But I'm ready to meet our baby."

Luna stands up and hugs me. "Just don't have the baby on Christmas. It won't be the same at my parents' without you guys."

Cam gives me a wave from the other seat past Luna. "Hey, Dani. Nathan, how's it going?"

Nathan looks grumpy. He leans over though and shakes Cam's hand. "Good. How about you?"

Cam tosses a hot, intense look at Luna. "Never better."

I love that my best friend has found her guys. It makes me beam at them.

"I just realized that I'm going to be sandwiched between two madly-in-love couples all night," Elise says, shaking her head in amusement. "This should be fun for me."

I sit down and turn to her. "So nothing has happened with Justin?" Elise confessed in a text to me and Luna back in August that she hooked up with Justin Travers after the Feeling Pucky event.

"Who?" Elise asks wryly.

"Justin Travers. Or as Crew likes to call him, Justin Fucking Travers. You know, from the Dallas Dragons."

Elise waves her hand. "Nah. That was a one-time thing when he was in town. No budding romance there." She grins. "Just hot sex. When does your book come out? I may need a manual on how to find multiple men willing to meet my every whim."

That makes me laugh. "Well, it is *fiction*, remember?" With a little dash of personal experience. "But I did the edits that the publisher wanted and now I'm just waiting. It's supposed to release in May."

"That's so exciting."

"It's awesome," Luna says, patting my knee. "I'm so proud of you, Dani."

"Thanks, Luna. Likewise. You're killing it with Books and Buns. Elise, what's new with you?"

She smiles. "Oh, not much."

We chit chat a little about Christmas plans and the baby and then the puck drops. Play has barely started when Nathan is texting on his phone. He leans over to me. "I'll be right back. There are some VIPs I need to go talk to. Are you going to be okay?"

"Yes, of course."

"You sure?"

"Yes." I turn to Luna. "Reassure Nathan you won't let me out of your sight while he's gone."

Luna leans over me. "Nathan, let this poor woman exist for five minutes without you hovering over her."

Nathan stares at her. Luna just calmly stares back.

Finally, he gives up with a sigh and stands up. "I'll be right back."

He leaves and Luna shakes her head. "I don't know how you can take it. He's on top of you all the time."

I just laugh. "I like it. I can't help it."

Cam stands up.

Luna swivels her head. "Where are you going? We just got here and you're leaving me already?"

His eyebrows shoot up. "To get your popcorn and your Diet Coke," he says calmly. "Like I do every game."

"Oh. Thank you."

He shakes his head with a smirk. "Sexy little hypocrite."

She makes a face at him.

Cam moves past us, and I awkwardly try to turn to shift my belly out of his way.

Elise grins. "He makes a fair point, Luna."

She grumbles. "Fine. Okay. I get it. When you love someone, you like them being around you."

I'm shifting around, trying to get comfortable in the seat. My back is tight. Christmas music is blaring over the speakers when there's a break in play, and I see Sammy the Malamute dancing to it with a Santa hat on his dog head.

Then without warning, Crew takes a shot and the puck lands in the net.

"Oh! Yes!" I shift to cheer and clap.

That's when it happens.

A warm gush right between my thighs. It takes a second for it to register, but then there is no mistaking it. My entire panties are wet and I feel an intense pressure in my lower back. Swallowing hard, I realize with excitement and a small amount of trepidation that my water has broken.

"Uh, Luna?"

"Hmm?" She drags her gaze off of her boyfriend Alexsei on the ice and turns to me.

"My water just broke."

Her jaw drops. "Are you shitting me?"

I shake my head.

"Okay. Holy shit. Let me text Nathan and Michael. Michael can tell Crew." She whips her phone out and starts texting rapidly.

"Should I boil water?" Elise asks with wide eyes. "Oh my God, this is so exciting! What can I do?"

"Can you magically produce me a change of clothes?" I ask,

only half-kidding. "My pants are soaked now. I'm embarrassed to stand up."

Elise whips off her sweater, revealing a tank top. "Here, tie this around your waist when you stand up. We don't need anyone snapping pics of your wet booty."

"Thank you." I take it gratefully and look at Luna. "Did Nathan respond?"

She shakes her head. "No. Let's just head up to his office and wait for him."

That makes me laugh a little. "He made me promise I wouldn't give birth in the arena."

"We have plenty of time. We'll get you to the hospital," she says, giving my arm a squeeze. "I'm texting my mom. She can go to your house and pick up your hospital bag and meet us there."

I put my hands on my cheeks. "I'm having a baby. I am having a baby. This is happening." I shift in the seat and the pressure on my back gets worse. "Jesus, I don't think I can stand up."

Luna shocks me by putting her fingers to her mouth and giving a sharp whistle. She waves her arms wildly. "Hey! Sammy! Get your furry butt over here."

The mascot looks at us, looks to his left and then his right, like he assumes Luna is talking to someone else.

"Yes, you!" She gestures for him to come over. "We need you."

Sammy bounds up the couple of steps and skids to a halt in front of us.

"Help Dani up. She's in labor."

His paw goes to his mouth then he gives a nod, his costume head jiggling a little. He rips his paw glove off and holds his hand out to me.

I almost laugh. Except I'm afraid if I laugh I'll make the wet-pant-situation worse. I tie Elise's sweater around my waist and take Sammy's hand. He's stronger than he looks. He manages to haul me up and out into the aisle, his grip steady and reassuring. I give him a grateful smile as he starts to walk me up the steps.

Luna hovers on my other side and Elise brings up the rear, holding our coats and purses.

Fans are eyeing me curiously so I give them a smile and remind myself women do this every minute of every day and I have no reason to panic.

The announcer is saying, "We have a substitution, folks. Looks like number seventeen is heading to the locker room."

That immediately makes me feel better. Michael must have seen Luna's text and told Crew. They're leaving the game.

Cam is at the top of the stairs holding Luna's snacks. "What's going on?"

"Dani's water broke."

He gives a look of alarm, then shoves the popcorn at Sammy. "Here, take this. I've got Dani."

Sammy lets go of me and takes the popcorn. He lifts his mask and for the first time I see the real person in the mascot costume. Wade looks a little younger than me, with kind eyes and a bright smile. "Yo, good luck," he says. "You've got this."

"Thanks, Wade. I appreciate your help."

"No problem." His gaze has already drifted to Elise's substantial cleavage, rising high out of her tank top.

She shakes her head. "No. There's nothing in there for you, dog boy."

He gives a sheepish shrug and tosses some popcorn in his mouth. "Sometimes you gotta look directly into the sun."

With that, he wanders back down the stairs, dropping his mascot head back into place.

It makes me giggle, maybe slightly hysterically. The pain is intensifying faster than I imagined. I'm half hunched over, death grip on Cam's hand.

"What the fuck was that?" Luna asks, shaking her head. She puts her phone to her ear. "I'm calling Nathan. Cam, let's get Dani to the elevator."

It's a slow walk but we make it to the elevator that goes up to the private suites and offices. I'm asking Luna to dig around in my bag for my security clearance pass to access it when the doors glide open and Nathan strides out, his expression stormy.

"Thank God," he breathes when he sees me. "Are you okay?"

I nod. "My water broke and my back hurts. *Really* bad."

Cam releases me and Nathan strides forward, pulling me against him, his hand going to my lower back to massage beneath Elise's sweater. "I told you it was a bad idea to come to the game."

"This is an excellent time for an I-told-you-so," Luna says, rolling her eyes as she texts on her phone. "Just call your driver to pick you two up. We'll meet you at the hospital."

"I want to wait for Michael and Crew," I say.

Nathan looks like he's about to argue, but then he just nods shortly.

Michael suddenly appears beside me. "Cookie. You okay?" He looks a little nervous, but sounds calm.

"Yes. Where's Crew?"

"He's probably changing. He can meet us at the hospital."

"No. I want to wait," I say stubbornly. "We need to go together."

Then I see him. My sweet, loyal, amazing other husband, rushing down the hallway, still in his uniform. He has sneakers on his feet and he's taken off his helmet and gloves, but otherwise he's still in full gear, jogging toward us.

Relief courses through me.

"This is it?" he asks with a confident grin. "It's go time? Fuck yeah."

I smile at my husbands. "Let's go have a baby."

CHAPTER 24
Nathan

I'M ANNOYING DANIELLE. I know I am. I can feel it. I hear it in my own voice how overbearing and anxious I sound. Hell, I'm annoying myself.

Yet I can't seem to stop.

I'm both excited and scared to death.

Seeing Danielle hooked up to all the monitors has really driven home for me what I haven't given much thought to before today—something could go wrong.

I haven't *let* myself think about that.

Because Danielle's pregnant. There's no avoiding all of this. So I've just pushed all of the 'bad things happen in hospitals all the fucking time' to the back of my mind.

Until now.

I don't remember a lot about the night of the car accident that killed my parents. I was unconscious for a lot of it. But I do remember waking up in a hospital in pain. I remember the white walls, bright lights, people in scrubs, and beeping monitors.

I suppressed so much of it, but I know that's part of what's feeding my anxiety now.

That and the trips to the ER and the admissions for my grandfather when his dementia was progressing but before he was placed in assisted living.

And the visits to my grandmother before her death.

And now my *wife*, the person I love more than anything on earth, is in one of those fucking beds, hooked up to monitors, and everyone's acting like all of this is no big deal because they see it every day.

"Take it down a notch," Michael says to me under his breath for about the fourth time. But this time he adds, "You're not helping Dani."

I just barked at a nurse who told us Danielle can't have an epidural yet because she's not dilated enough.

"I just hate hospitals."

I can't stand hospitals and I hate seeing the woman I love in pain even more. It's just about killing me that I can't make this go any faster or easier for Danielle.

We've been here approximately nine hundred hours at this point. Or three. One of the two. It just feels like this is taking forever and I have resorted to pacing while Danielle tries to sleep between contractions. Crew, who almost never sits still, has more nervous energy than even me and he trips for the second time, crashing into a bedside chart.

"Shit," he says, when Dani jerks awake at the noise. "Sorry, baby."

"Why do you keep tripping?" I ask him. I look at his feet. "Are those the shoes you left the house in?"

He's stripped off his pads but is still in his jersey. Lori McNeill dropped off Danielle's overnight bag, but she didn't realize Crew needed a change of clothes. She said she would have William bring him something but so far Crew's father hasn't arrived.

"No, they are not. I don't know whose shoes these are," Crew admits. "I think they might be Wilder's. He has big fucking feet. I didn't want to waste time so I just grabbed the first pair of shoes in the locker room I saw sitting out."

"Oh, Jesus," Michael says, shaking his head as he smoothes a blanket down over Danielle. "You had time to change. Or at least open your locker and get your own shoes."

"I think it's sweet," Danielle murmurs, her eyes closed.

She looks tired already and hard labor hasn't even started. So far, all of her labor has been primarily in her back and she keeps tossing and turning trying to find a comfortable position. I was kneading her back for a while, but she pushed me away. Now I just feel helpless and frustrated.

"I'm sweet," Crew tells me, with a grin.

Aside from the fact that he can't sit still, he's been very calm during this whole thing. Irritatingly calm. Danielle seems to be gravitating towards him and while it's not a competition, it still makes me feel inadequate. I want to be there for my wife and instead, I'm snapping at nurses and wearing a path in the linoleum.

The monitor beeps.

"What does that mean?" I demand, reaching out and smacking Michael on the arm. "Is everything okay?"

"Everything is fine. It's just turning her blood pressure cuff on."

Michael looks and sounds calm, but there is a rigidity in his shoulders that I don't usually see. He's trying to be soothing for Danielle, but he's nervous, too. This is a big deal. A baby is about to make its entrance into the world.

Our baby.

That has me moving forward to push an errant and sweaty curl out of Danielle's face. "Do you need anything?"

"I need you to not touch me right now," she says.

I drop my hand from her immediately.

Crew is sweet and I'm not allowed to touch her. I try to make my tone mimic Michael's. "Whatever you say, sweetheart."

"How about an ice chip?" Michael asks, fishing one out of a cup with a plastic spoon.

"Just stop hovering over me. Please."

We look at each other and both back slowly away from the bed.

"How about some music?" Crew asks, fiddling with his phone. Suddenly, rap music blasts from it loudly. "Shit, sorry. Wrong playlist."

"Crew!" Danielle snaps. "Turn that off."

He immediately obeys and clears his throat. He plops down on a chair.

Another nurse comes into the room and eyes all of us with confusion. "Shift change," she says. "I'm Mariah. Which one of you gentlemen is Dad?"

I'm about to open my mouth to say we all are, when I realize that's overcomplicating things and Danielle doesn't need overcomplicated.

Crew and I both gesture to Michael. "He is," I tell her.

Crew stands up and steps back to allow the nurse to move forward toward the bed. "Yep, he's your guy."

We know it now for a fact. We had a DNA test done about six weeks ago in preparation for Danielle's birth plan, just for the legalities of it all. Michael is the biological father of our baby. Crew handled the news well and Michael has never made us feel like we weren't a part of what is happening just because it's him that actually made this baby with Danielle. We all talked openly and honestly about it and we assured Danielle there would be no egos in the birthing room, and I'm determined to honor that promise.

Not that it's hard for me regarding the biological thing. Not really. I've always known the baby wasn't mine. There's been a certain freedom for me in that knowledge.

"I'm Dr. Michael Hughes," Michael says. "The father."

"Excellent. I'll need the two of you to step out while I examine Danielle's cervix." She gives me and Crew a shooing motion with a smile.

My first instinct is to push back but then I look at Danielle. She's wincing in pain. I hesitate, not sure what she wants. Then I realize this is something I do have control over. I can make the decision for her. Crew obviously feels the same way because he's already heading for the door.

"Come on," he says to me. "Let's take a walk. We can grab a cup of coffee."

Considering Crew doesn't even drink coffee, I know he's just saying that to let Danielle know we'll be gone for a little while.

She clearly needs some space right now.

I glance at Michael. "Text us if you need to."

He nods. "Of course. Dani, do you want me to leave too?"

She reaches for his hand. "No. Please stay. I need you to listen to all the medical stuff. I can't seem to think right now."

Crew and I step out into the hallway. "I'm going to have a heart attack," I tell him, rubbing my forehead. "This is fucking hard. I hate seeing her in pain."

He just gives me his signature grin. "It's gonna be fine. Dani's got this. Come on, Nate." He claps me on the shoulder. "Let's just give our girl some space."

"I'm not very good at that."

"No shit."

We walk off down the hall, Crew clomping in his borrowed shoes, and I feel like I left my whole entire heart in that room.

CHAPTER 25
Crew

"LET'S GO THIS WAY," I say, turning left.

I know the Boss is tense. Tonight is an unusual night. It's unusual for us to see Dani in pain. We've seen her upset, tense, worried, even sick with a cold or morning sickness, but I don't think any of us have ever actually seen her in physical pain. Nothing like this anyway.

It's tough. I'm not gonna lie.

But she's here, where people can take care of her. And Doc's right by her side, watching the monitors, talking to the nurses and doctors. If there were any problems, he would know. And he would take care of it.

Our girl is a little snappish. I don't blame her. I know how it feels to have pain digging at you, taking over your rational thought processes, and how annoying it can be, when people are hovering, trying to help, but mostly just being in the way.

We have to be here. We *want* to be here. But obviously, Nathan and I are useless. Except for emotional support, of course. But it's clear that Dani is past the point where she needs us telling her she's amazing or that she's doing great or that everything will be over soon.

I'm not even sure how helpful Michael's really being, but at least he can decipher the medical stuff, and I know that makes her feel more secure, but the dude knows about hips and shoulders, not sure he knows that much about babies.

Still, he's the calm one. He's the soothing one.

There are lots of positive adjectives I know everyone around us would use for both Nathan and I.

Calm and soothing are not the ones, though.

"You gotta stop," Nathan says to me.

He sounds tired. I look over. "Stop what?"

"The humming."

I didn't realize I was humming. I grin. "Sorry. Not intentional."

He gives me a puzzled look. "How are you humming? You're in a really good mood."

I stop and face him. I know I must look surprised. "Of course I'm in a good mood."

"Danielle, your *wife*, is in that room in excruciating pain and you can't do anything about it. How does that put you in a good mood?"

I can't help it, I grin. "*Nathan*, on the other side of this, we're gonna have a baby. The next time we walk through our front door, it's gonna be with a little Dani or Michael. This is just the start to an amazing adventure. And..." I study Nathan's face, trying to decide if he's actually ready for what I'm about to say. Then I decide I don't care. "I get to go on this adventure with my three best friends. Dads my age are probably terrified. I'm not. You know why? Because my kid is going to have the most amazing mother ever. And that's even over Lori McNeill. Though if you tell her that I'll deny it. And I'm not worried about anything because my kid is going to have you and Michael. Anything I can't do, anything I screw up, you guys will be there to fix. That's fucking amazing." I spread my arms wide. "This is one of the best days of my fucking life. And I've had a pretty damned good life so far, so that's saying something."

Nathan is staring at me. But the frown lines on his forehead have eased up.

"But Dani..."

I drop my arms and nod. "Man, I know. It's tough to see her go through this. But she'll be okay. Michael will make sure of that. The two of us don't have to do anything but stand around and be cocky about that amazing woman choosing us. That baby at the end of the day is going to be *ours*. We're the luckiest sons of bitches in this hospital." I take a breath and blow it out, feeling so fucking...*happy*. This is just pure joy. "And Dani can handle this, Nathan. She's in pain, for sure. But she's stronger than you realize. Than any of us give her credit for sometimes. Let her prove that to us. Let her go through this. Let her prove it to *herself*. And you know she's excited. She wants this baby so much. I promise, when this is over, Dani's going to be a new person. And believe it or not, I think she's going to be even more incredible than she was before. So maybe you should just take this time to get ready for that. Because even being in the same room with that gorgeous angel is gonna be a lot for a couple of dumbasses like us."

Again, Nathan just stares at me for several long moments. Then he blows out of breath. "Fuck, it's good to have you back."

I let out a surprise chuckle. "What do you mean?"

"This. This is what you're good at. This is why we all need you. At least one of the really big reasons. After the championship loss, you sank into yourself and were sad and pissed off and frustrated. And that's fine," he says quickly. "I'm not saying that it's not. But it's not you. You're the happy, optimistic, annoyingly positive, fun guy. We all need you to bring this... *happy* into our lives." He pauses. "We missed you."

Now *I'm* staring at him like an idiot. "Nathan Armstrong," I say. "Are you saying that you love me?"

He rolls his eyes, but he says, "Yes McNeill, I'm saying that I love you."

I clap him on the shoulder. "Fuck yeah you do. And I love you. Now come on, I've got something to show you."

We continue down the hallway past another set of doors, and then I spread my arms. "Check this out."

Nathan steps up to the window, his eyes wide.

He's looking in on the nursery. There are about a dozen babies in there right now. And they're cute as fuck.

"We're gonna have one of those, Boss. Soon. Our girl is giving us one of those right now."

He nods, and I realize that at the moment, he can't speak.

So I just pat him on the shoulder again.

"See, best day of our life."

CHAPTER 26
Michael

THE LABOR IS GOING AS WELL AS can be expected. First babies take their sweet time and Dani is progressing as she should. All her vitals are good. It's just a waiting game. A long, hard, emotional waiting game.

Being a physician isn't really helping me other than I can readily read Dani's monitors and the body language of the nurses and the doctor, who has only been in the room once. Everyone looks like this is business as usual so I'm not concerned.

But I've never been in a labor and delivery room. It's one thing to think about it intellectually, another to be here, in this moment, seeing my wife go through all the phases of labor, pain etched on her features.

I feel like I'm walking a tightrope, trying to gauge what Dani needs and doesn't need from me. That of course is nothing compared to what she's enduring so I put aside my own discomfort and just try to listen and respond accordingly. At one point, she was leaning against me, letting me cradle her. Then she was shoving me away, saying she was hot.

Now she's shivering and the nurse is putting a heated blanket over her. I know that indicates she's in the transition phase of labor and we're getting really close. She's moaning low in the back of her throat in spite of having an epidural.

Crew and Nathan came back after their walk more relaxed and that seemed to help Dani relax more as well.

She did snap at them once when they were watching a video on Crew's phone but since then we've taken turns rotating in and out of her bedside. She doesn't have a preference for any of us. We've equally gotten her irritation, her tears, and her outstretched hand seeking comfort.

The nurse has side-eyed us a few times and is probably wondering who Crew and Nathan are, but she's a professional and hasn't asked. Truthfully, she probably doesn't care. I don't feel the need to explain either. Our family is our business and we've only grown stronger the last few months.

Dani needed Crew to marry her. She only feels complete with all of us together and we work. We're a solid unit and I love that. I also love that neither Nathan nor Crew batted an eye when the DNA results matched to me. I would have loved this baby no matter what, but I am looking forward to seeing a blend of me and Dani together in this child. A book-loving, calm kid.

Watch this baby somehow have Crew's energy and Nathan's attitude in spite of genetics.

Crew is holding up a plastic pan for Dani, who is now dry heaving. He's smoothing her hair back and she's so tired she isn't even brushing him off. When she settles back, she's quiet, focused internally on working with her body.

"I'm so proud of you," I tell her. "You're doing great."

"I don't know if I can do this," she says, panting and clawing at the bedrail as another contraction hits her. "My back, Michael. Oh, my God. It hurts so bad. Why the fuck isn't this epidural working?"

"Just breathe, sweetheart. Don't fight it. Lean into it. Relax your shoulders and just breathe in your nose and out your mouth."

I've lost track of what time it is.

My mom and my sister are en route from Decatur. Lori and Luna are still in the waiting room and Crew's father showed up with shoes that actually fit him, which was a relief. We don't need him taking a spill right in the middle of the action. Not to mention Nathan would kill him if he got injured mid-season.

It has to be around two in the morning, which isn't really that long for a first time mom. Not that I'm stupid enough to say that to Dani. She would probably throw me out of the room if I suggested in any way that she's fortunate things have been moving quickly. It's clear now that she's been in labor at least a day or two, but it was all in her back. She's had so much back pain it didn't register as anything different and she wasn't due for an OB/GYN appointment for another three days.

All in all, everything is going great and probably within the hour, the baby will be born.

The nurse confirms it when she checks Dani. "Almost time. I'm going to let the doctor know." She pats Dani's hand. "Just try to relax. If you feel the need to push, don't bear down just yet, okay? We want the doctor here for baby."

Dani manages a nod. But the second the nurse leaves the room, she says urgently, "Michael. I need to push."

She's struggling to sit up so I grab her elbow and help her get into a more upright position. "Just breathe, don't push yet. You can do this."

"I can't stop it!" She moans a little, her knees falling apart. "Oh, God."

Nathan pushes the nurse call button before I can stop him. There is pure panic on his face.

Crew moves into action and rushes to Dani's other side and takes her hand. "Just squeeze my hand. Push on me instead of... down there."

That almost makes me laugh. That might be the first time I've ever heard Crew McNeill at a loss for words when it comes to Dani's body.

I shift Dani's hospital gown up her thighs and I see the baby crowning.

I wasn't expecting that. Things are really moving. "You're doing great. Try not to push, Cookie. Just hold off for another minute."

"All of you stop telling me not to push! I can't help it!" Dani grits her teeth, her eyes squeezing shut.

She's clearly pushing. Yep. It's happening.

Quickly, I go over to the sink and wash my hands thoroughly, just in case. Nathan actually looks like he might pass out. But even though he momentarily loses all color in his face when he sees the baby's head, he pulls himself together and takes Dani's other side, stuffing another pillow behind her so she's fully sitting up.

"You're doing great," he tells her. "Almost time." He shoots me a what-the-fuck look.

I know what he's thinking—where the hell is the doctor? Because I'm thinking it too. But to his credit, he doesn't say it out loud, knowing it will scare Dani. I glance toward the door, wondering if I dare risk going out into the hallway to find out what the delay is.

But then the doctor strolls in, all casual. She takes one look at the situation and gives me a smile. "Well, okay. It looks like we're ready to have a baby, Danielle."

A nurse is right on her heels.

The next few minutes are a blur of shifting Dani down on the bed, instructions from the doctor to Dani, and counting through the pushes during contractions.

Then just like that, the baby is in the doctor's hands, giving an immediate cry.

I suck in a deep breath, overcome with emotion.

Dani leans forward. "What is it?" she asks. "Is everything okay?"

"You have a baby girl. And she looks perfect. Congratulations!"

"A girl?" Dani beams as the doctor passes our daughter up to her, taking her in her arms and holding her close to her chest. "Oh, my goodness. Hi, little darling."

Seeing my two girls together has my eyes filling with tears. I lean in and run my hand down my daughter's back. "She's perfect. Beautiful like her mama." I stare in awe at her stocky little body, the tufts of hair on her head, her tiny little fists balled up as she cries. I give Dani a kiss on the forehead. "You did fantastic, Dani. I love you."

"I love you too." She smiles up at me, then immediately her gaze returns to our daughter.

Nathan smoothes Dani's hair back from her forehead. He is openly crying, without reservation or embarrassment. I hold my hand out to him and he gives it a firm shake, nodding, like he is so happy he can't speak.

"A girl," Crew murmurs, his finger lightly stroking over the top of the baby's head. "Look at her... she's amazing." He's misty-eyed too.

The only one of us not crying is Dani. She is beaming, all her fatigue replaced by the joy of holding our daughter. Her eyes are bright with love, her mouth turned up in a soft smile. She cradles the baby, kissing the top of her head. "Michael, look, she has your eyes."

She turns the baby a little for me to see. The baby's eyes are big and unblinking. She gives a tiny yawn. I can't see that she really looks like either of us right now. She just looks like a newborn baby to me, but I nod.

"Does she have a name?" the nurse asks.

Dani looks from me to Nathan to Crew, giving each of us a loving smile. "Yes."

We had all agreed that since the baby will have my last name, the first name should be a tribute to Nathan's mom or dad, depending on the gender. The middle name was for Dani and Crew to choose together, and after Crew tossed around absurd ideas like Seventeen, after his hockey number, or Crewelle, a mash up of their names, they told us they had settled on a flower if it was a girl but kept it a secret.

Dani announces now, "This is Isabel Poppy Hughes."

It's the perfect blend of all four of us. If I had chosen a flower name I would have gone traditional. Rose or Lily. But Poppy is just like Crew and Dani together—bright and vibrant and joyous.

"I love it," I tell her.

Crew nods. "It's a solid name."

"Thank you," Nathan tells Dani. "For you. For this. For Isabel."

"Don't forget to take pictures," the nurse tells us cheerfully.

I take a few pictures of Dani and the baby and close ups of Isabel.

"Can you take one of all four of us?" Dani asks her.

"Sure."

I hand her my phone and we crowd around the bed, leaning in around our girl on all sides, a complete family. Nathan with red eyes, Crew still is his jersey grinning, me, the proud puffed-up-chest father. Dani, glowing with pride and love.

The nurse shows Crew the shot while Dani passes the baby to me to hold. I stare down at her tiny perfection, feeling more than I ever imagined it could be possible to feel. "Welcome to the world, Isabel. You're going to love it here," I tell her.

CHAPTER 27
Dani

"I'M NOT WEARING THIS," Nathan says as he stumbles down the stairs, hair sticking up, plucking at the T-shirt he has on. "Otherwise, Merry Christmas."

"You clearly *are* wearing it," Michael says, blowing on the tea he's made for me as he carries it over and sets it on the end table next to me. "And Merry Christmas to you too, Nathan."

"Thank you," I tell Michael with a smile as I nurse Isabel in the club chair next to the couch. I love the couch almost as much as Crew does but it's not practical for breastfeeding. I smooth a finger down my daughter's tiny cheek, in awe every time I look at her, which is every chance I get.

She's absolutely beautiful and perfect and she completes our family. I'm tired and a little sore, but I've never been happier.

Nathan is struggling to get over the baby gate. He looks exhausted. He hasn't slept much at all in the two days since we brought Isabel home from the hospital. He gets up to help me with diaper changes and to keep me company when I'm nursing throughout the night but I also secretly think he's afraid if he sleeps he'll miss too much. Or maybe that if he sleeps he'll wake up and this will have all been a dream.

I understand and appreciate him, but I wish he would sleep.

He looks more than a little grumpy. Crew's gift from last night isn't helping. Crew gave us all silly Christmas T-shirts and matching red plaid pajama pants to wear while we eat breakfast and open presents this morning.

I think it's adorable.

Nathan does not.

My T-shirt, which I am happily wearing, says "Christmas Cookie." Michael's says "Daddy Claus." The one Crew got for himself reads "Christmas Crew" and Isabel's red onesie says "Best. Gift. Ever." which we all absolutely agree on.

Nathan's shirt says, "Christmas Grinch."

Which Crew finds hilarious.

"It's a gift," Crew says, coming into the living room wearing his pajamas and carrying a glass of orange juice. "You can't reject a gift. It's rude."

Nathan still hasn't made it over the baby gate. He's been trying to undo the latch. He rattles it in irritation then sighs and climbs over it, using the railing for support.

"Are you okay, Nathan?" I ask in a soft voice. "You don't have to wear the shirt."

"Yes, he does," Crew protests.

Michael gives Crew a look.

Crew immediately relents. "She's right, Nate. You don't have to wear it. I was just trying to have some fun."

Now Nathan looks sheepish. He comes over and kisses the top of my head. "I'm wonderful. Seriously. This is the best Christmas I've ever had in my entire life. I'm just a little tired."

I unlatch Isabel and lift her to gently pat her back. Nathan immediately reaches out. "Can I take her?"

"Of course."

We do the transfer and he rests her against his chest, closing his eyes briefly and sighing. Tears spring up in my eyes. Seeing Nathan as a father is beautiful.

Michael has cinnamon rolls baking in the oven. Our gas fireplace is pumping out heat and our Christmas tree is tall and proud, twinkling merrily. Snow is gently drifting down onto our street and it's picture perfect. It's a Hallmark movie. If Hallmark movies had poly romances in them.

Nathan is gently swaying. "I love the shirt," he tells Crew. "And I'm not even mad that I'm wearing the matching pants with you and Michael."

Crew lets out a laugh. "That almost killed you, didn't it?"

"Really close to death here. But if I'm going out, this is the way to do it."

Michael sees the tears in my eyes and he gives me a soft smile, bending over so we're eye level. "Do you need anything?"

That makes me sniffle, my throat tight. I reach for the tea he made me. "No. I have everything I could ever want."

"Me too." He gives me a light kiss before standing back up. "I should shovel the driveway before it gets too deep. Everyone's coming over at two, right?"

I nod. "Yes. The whole family. Even my parents. They're excited to meet Isabel."

The McNeills will be here, Val, Michael's parents and siblings and his nieces and nephews. He was worried it would be too much for me, but I'm looking forward to seeing everyone and letting the whole extended family see the baby, without us having to leave our house. Everyone is bringing a potluck dish, which is a foreign concept to Nathan, who wanted to cater it, but I prefer the love that comes with the whole family pitching in.

"Let me shovel," Crew says. "I haven't worked out in five days. I'll do a quick pass and then we can eat, right? I'm going to destroy those cinnamon rolls."

That makes me smile. Crew is always thinking about his stomach.

"I need some coffee. Badly." Nathan turns to Michael. "Here, your turn."

"Isabel needs to nurse on the other side," I tell him.

Michael nods. "Just give me a second with her."

I sip my tea as Nathan stumbles into the kitchen.

Michael has the baby in a football hold so he can see her face. "Merry Christmas, angel. Yes, it's your first Christmas. What do you think?" His voice is low and soothing as he talks and makes faces at her. "I love you." He looks back at me. "And I love *you*."

Michael as a father is strong and steady, as always, our whiskey smooth voice of reason.

Isabel is wearing the graphic onesie and tiny red plaid pants with a knit red cap on her head to keep her warm. Her little fingers are curled up.

"Oh, her sock is coming off." Crew is there in a flash to secure her sock back on her little foot. He kisses her heel first before tugging the cotton sock back up and then makes a goofy face at her. "No cold babies on Daddy three's watch."

I love how Crew's face softens when he looks at Isabel. It's a mixture of awe and adoration. It makes me fall in love with him even more.

I'm falling in love with all three of my husbands deeper and with more appreciation every second I see them spending with our daughter, loving her, caring for her, protecting her.

Nathan returns with a coffee mug in his hand. He's cradling it and staring out our front window blankly. "It's snowing," as if the other guys hadn't just been discussing that.

Michael bends down. "Ready for her?"

"Yes." I take the baby from him and smile at her sweet little face. She's awake and shifting her head around.

"White Christmas," Crew declares. "The only thing that would make today even better would be if we had that RV."

Nathan gives a sly smile behind his mug.

It immediately makes me suspicious. I catch Michael's eye but he shrugs.

Then with perfect timing, we hear a horn beep. Crew goes to the window. Immediately, his hands go to his head.

"It's here," he murmurs, like it's a Christmas miracle. "The RV." He turns and gives us a grin. "Nate. You sentimental bastard."

Nathan looks incredibly pleased with himself.

Now I'm grinning too. "You didn't."

"I did."

Michael goes to the window too. "Did you *buy* this thing?"

"I did. Cookie & Co. tradition, right? That's what it's all about. Family and traditions."

"Best. Christmas. Ever," Crew says.

"Best life ever," Michael says.

"Best family ever," Nathan adds.

I snuggle our daughter to my chest.

I couldn't agree more.

Epilogue

Six Months Later
Nathan

"COME ON, COME ON," I murmur under my breath. "Just hold them off." My knee is bouncing up and down and Danielle puts her hand on it.

Her touch always calms me, but all I can do is offer her a brief smile right now before glancing back at the ice. The Racketeers are up 3-2 against the Dragons in the championship game and there's only thirty seconds of game time left. The Dragons are on a power play and our coach just called a timeout. If the Dragons score here I'm going to have to suffer through overtime.

"Relax," Stanford says, sipping the world's largest slushie in his seat next to me. He looks like a million bucks, wearing an Armani suit, his hair and eyebrows carefully tamed by a stylist this afternoon.

His nurse and Val are next to him, just in case, but he's mostly lucid today. Except for the moments when he seems to think he's much younger and his nurse is actually his girlfriend. Fortunately, Chrissy seems used to it and plays along with him.

"How can you be so calm?" I ask him.

"I've got one foot in the grave, Nathan," he says. "What's there to get worked up about?"

That makes me chuckle. "Fair enough."

We're in the owner's box because I wanted my grandfather to be here. Isabel as well. When we're in the stands, we put noise canceling headphones on the baby, but up here we don't have to worry about the crowd. She slept through the majority of the third period, but is sitting on Danielle's lap now, dressed in Racketeers gear Crew had specially made by an Etsy vendor. It's a onesie with Sammy the Malamute's face on it and Crew's number, seventeen, on the back. There's a blue tutu around her round belly and Sammy tights on her legs. Her socks are designed to look like hockey skates.

Crew has become the dad who wants our daughter in theme clothing all the time. Michael and Danielle go for practical outfits most of the time, and I have a bad habit of buying her ridiculously over-the-top things like Baby Dior. But Crew brings the fun and has Isabel decked out for every holiday and occasion in something adorably kitschy. She was the cutest leprechaun to ever exist on St. Patrick's Day. Right now, she has a giant bow perched on her beautiful dark curls and she is a little glassy-eyed, up way past her bedtime.

"McNeill's having a great game," my grandfather says.

"He is," Danielle says, her voice filled with pride. "He's worked so hard this season."

I don't comment because the puck drops.

Our guys are doing everything to prevent the Dragons from taking a shot and to burn down the clock. I'm on the edge of my seat. Harris won't be out of the box until regulation is up. But then the best possible thing happens—Alexsei Ryan steals the puck from their forward and passes it to Crew.

I jump up out of my seat and yell in encouragement.

McNeill takes it down the ice and evades their defenseman, who tries to slam him into the glass. That doesn't work and Crew is skating hard to the goal, he gets intentionally tripped but somehow manages to stay on his feet. The foul is called, but there's only ten seconds left on the clock.

Miraculously, Crew manages to get off a shot right before the buzzer and it sails past their goalie into the net, securing the win.

My grandfather surges to his feet beside me, slushie still in hand. I'm clapping, in awe.

This is it. We did it.

The guys pulled it off.

We fucking *did it!*

Crew is being hoisted up by his teammates and the whole bench is out on the ice now.

I turn to Danielle. I can feel how huge my grin is. I can't believe all of the emotions tumbling around inside me. "Holy shit. We *won*."

She's on her feet too, beaming, tears in her eyes. "This is amazing!"

I cup the back of her head and pull her in for a kiss. She meets my lips, but we don't have time for a long kiss. I let her go. "I love you."

"I love you too! I'm so happy for you." She looks down and bounces Isabel up and down. "We won, baby!"

Even Isabel looks a little stunned, like she can't believe this is happening.

Fans are screaming, the roar deafening. Ticker tape in the Racketeers colors is raining down and Wade, in his Sammy the Malamute costume, is breakdancing on the ice.

My grandfather takes my hand and gives it a firm shake that nearly breaks my heart. "You did it, son," he says. "Congratulations."

"Thank you. This is all for you, you know? This is your legacy." I can barely get the words out. "This city has had hockey for fifty years because of *you* and I promise you, the Racketeers will still be here fifty years from now."

Stanford nods. Then he reaches over and tickles Isabel's belly and gives Danielle a kiss on the cheek. "This is my legacy, too," he says. "Your family. I'm proud of you, Nathan, and your father would be too."

That's all I need. Now I truly have everything a man could ever want.

I turn and hug Val, who gives me a big smacking kiss on the cheek. "Congratulations, Nathan!"

"I just…" Suddenly I can't speak.

She pats my cheek. "I know."

Ten minutes later, we've left Stanford and Val in the box and made our way down to the ice. There are interviews and hand-shaking and cheers all around. Michael and Crew find us, and Crew immediately takes Isabel, her noise canceling headphones back on, and hoists her up in the air. She rewards him with a squeal and a giggle. Michael gives Danielle a kiss and then she leans in to press one to Crew's lips as well. "I'm so proud of you," she tells him, tears spilling over. "I love you."

"I love you so much, Dani," he tells her, his eyes watery as well.

There's no thought to the future when right now is so damn perfect, but if I had to consider it, I see nothing but love and joy and an expanding family with Cookie & Co. I'm going to grow old with these two men and our wife, and however many children Danielle wants to have. Older than I am now, anyway, since Crew will never get tired of razzing me about my age.

I hold my hand out to him. He takes it with a grin. "Nice shot, right, Nate?"

"It was a great shot, McNeill. Worth every penny I've paid you. And maybe even worth putting up with that fucking couch." We both laugh. He knows I actually love that couch and I don't care that he knows. "Congratulations, Crew."

"I'll still expect a bonus and that pony you promised me."

I laugh again. I think I'm actually going to buy him a pony. Just to shut him up about it.

I shake Michael's hand next. "Thanks for your dedication to our players."

"It was an amazing season, Boss," he says.

A reporter shoves a microphone in my face. "Tell us what this championship means to you, Mr. Armstrong."

"What does this mean to me?" I repeat. I would typically give a short, practiced answer or pass the reporter off to a player, but tonight I want the microphone. I definitely have something to say. "I'll tell you exactly what this means to me. When I was six years old my grandfather brought me and my father down onto the ice after the Racketeers won their last championship. It wasn't this arena, of course, it was the old one they tore down twenty years ago. But he said we should be proud of being an Armstrong and that when the fourth generation son was standing next to us, there would be a whole row of pennants hanging from that ceiling." I draw in a deep breath. "Then my father died. I found out I can't have kids. And there were no more pennants, not for thirty-five very difficult and empty years."

I feel my family move in to surround me. Danielle squeezes my hand. Crew claps me on the shoulder. Michael passes Isabel over to me. I take her gratefully and I kiss the top of her head behind that ridiculous bow Crew picked out for her and I breathe in the scent of her tiny baby perfection. I clear my throat.

"And now? I have my amazing wife, Danielle, I have the incomparable Dr. Michael Hughes, star player Crew McNeill, and I have our beautiful daughter. My grandfather, Stanford Armstrong, was here to witness this win, and all our players have given something really special to the city of Chicago tonight. It means *everything* to me."

Danielle rubs the small of my back.

Her touch, her love, has completely transformed my life.

"So watch out, because this is the beginning of a hot streak."

"Thank you, Mr. Armstrong and congratulations to you and the whole team."

"Thank you." I grin. "Now let's party."

Crew gives a whoop.

Isabel gives me a gummy grin.

Michael nods in approval.

I turn to Danielle. "What do you think? Should we celebrate?"

She gives me a sweet but naughty smile. "You're the boss."

———

About Emma Foxx

Emma Foxx is the super fun and sexy pen name for two long-time, bestselling romance authors who decided why have just one hero when you can have three at the same time? (they're not sure what took them so long to figure this out)! Emma writes contemporary romances that will make you laugh (yes, maybe out loud in public) and want more…books (sure, that's what we mean 😉). Find Emma on Instagram, Tik Tok, and Goodreads.

Read More Emma Foxx

ICING IT

A fun spin-off in the Racketeers world featuring Luna, Crew's sister!

Sex is a fantastic stress reliever.

Or so I'm told by the two hot guys who offer to help me get over some of my work-induced anxiety by getting under *both* of them.

I say yes. For one night.

And proceed to have my world rocked. For three days.

I can *not* afford that kind of distraction. As fun as it was, I have a business to run, a loan to pay off, and a life to live that does not include any extra commitments or responsibilities. Especially not a golden retriever hockey player and a bossy billionaire who are probably in love with each other and want to make *me* the third in their long-term plans.

And let's not even talk about the *third* guy who wants to date me. He's my brother's coach. And twelve years older than me. But he's also a single dad to a pretty great teenage son, and his competence and gentlemanly behavior are really hard to resist.

Of course, there's also the not-so-gentlemanly things he says and does behind bedroom doors…

Then they all go and fall in love with me. Even though one of them is definitely not interested in making this a full-time foursome.

And the icing on top?

I've fallen for them, too. All of them.

How can I possibly choose?

Worse, how can I possibly walk away?

Icing It is a steamy, fun STANDALONE why-choose rom com! No cheating, and a guaranteed HEA!

Missed the first three books in the series?

Puck One Night Stands
Four Pucking Christmases
Seriously Pucked

Milton Keynes UK
Ingram Content Group UK Ltd.
UKHW010902080524
442402UK00004B/148